BELIEVING IN PROMISES

A CIRCLE OF FRIENDS NOVEL

By

CATHRYN CHANDLER

1

<u>Books in the Circle of Friends series:</u>

Believing in Dreams (April 2016)

Believing in Love   (May 2016)

Only One Dream (June, 2016)

Only One Love (August 2016)

Believing in Promises (April 2017)

Coming Soon!: Only One Promise (July 2017)

Contents

Prologue 9

Chapter One 13

Chapter Two 23

Chapter Three 31

Chapter Four 39

Chapter Five 47

Chapter Six 57

Chapter Seven 67

Chapter Eight 75

Chapter Nine 82

Chapter Ten 90

Chapter Eleven 98

Chapter Twelve 106

Chapter Thirteen 112

Chapter Fourteen 115

Chapter Fifteen 122

Chapter Sixteen 131

Chapter Seventeen 140

Chapter Eighteen 150

Chapter Nineteen 159

Chapter Twenty 161

Chapter Twenty-One 169

Chapter Twenty-Two 177

Chapter Twenty-Three...184

Chapter Twenty-Four...193

BELIEVING IN PROMISES

April 1854
Hills North of San Francisco

Prologue

"Here's to the nights that turned into mornings, with the friends that turned into family" ~ Anonymous

It was a beautiful day.

Abby Metler closed her eyes and raised her face to the sun. She'd enjoyed the ride from San Francisco and looked forward to seeing all the children on Lillian's ranch. Her cousin had bought the land and turned it into a real home for orphaned and abandoned children, and part of Abby's work was to look after them on her semi-monthly visits.

Usually she rode along with the supply wagon Lillian sent each month. But this time she'd been delayed, so took the shorter cross-country route on her own. With any luck, she'd catch the supply wagon just before it arrived at the ranch, and neither George Cowan, the ranch manager, nor his wife, Carrie, would know she'd made the trip by herself.

Again.

Loud slurping noises drew her attention to a shaded spot along the stream not far from where she was sitting. She smiled fondly at Marron, her big muscular stallion, with a coat the color of dark, rich chocolate. Bred and raised by Rayne, a close friend of Abby's who lived on a ranch a few days out of town, Marron was a magnificent horse and one of a kind, just like all of Rayne's stock.

For the moment he'd abandoned chomping on clumps of grass to lap up the cool water flowing in gentle ripples down the shallow riverbed. Abby enjoyed the peaceful sound as much as she did the sunshine. She adjusted her glasses and drew her knees to her chest, which was a great deal easier to do in the britches she was wearing than the petticoats and skirts she usually had on. It was too bad she didn't want to wrestle with putting her boots on and off, otherwise she would have put her toes in the water. She hadn't gone wading in a river since she'd left her hometown in Connecticut over a year ago, to come to California to look for her missing cousin in San Francisco.

Once Abby had found Lillian, and then fallen in love with the city next to a sparkling bay, and all its possibilities, she'd decided to stay too.

"Yieeeee! Go get him!"

The yell came from the trees lining the other side of the riverbank, shattering the peaceful moment. Abby didn't need to hear the second shout to know she was about to have some very unwelcome company. And judging by their bellowing, they were either after her, or more likely, Marron. Despite her clothes, which may have led them to believe she was a "he", Abby was sure they weren't interested in her. Which meant they wanted her horse, and meant to leave her on foot—or worse.

Without taking time to look for the source of the thrashing noises coming from across the river that were growing louder by the second, Abby launched herself over the twenty feet separating her from Marron. The stallion was standing still, his ears pricked up and his head turned toward the trees. He didn't move as Abby scrambled into the saddle, using a special rope attached into the leather to haul herself up.

A quick jerk of the reins and firm squeeze of her knees had Marron swiveling around and taking off just as the distinct sound of horses running through water came from behind them. Abby sent the big stallion at a wild pace through the trees, heading straight for the grasslands beyond the wooded sanctuary. She needed to get to open ground. Once there, the only way they'd ever catch Marron is if one of them was riding another of Rayne's horses. There were very few things Marron couldn't outrun.

But a bullet was one of them.

Bark exploded on a tree they'd just flown past, and Abby bent her body until she was lying flat along Marron's neck and back. It took one of the longest ten seconds of her life, but they finally burst out of the trees, and Marron instantly broke into an all-out run. More bullets flew around them, thudding into the ground until the big stallion finally gained enough distance the shooting stopped. At least they were no longer in target range of the men chasing them. But it didn't take long for Abby to realize where Marron was headed.

She couldn't bring horse thieves right up to the ranch's doorstep.

Abby sent her horse to the left, thinking that somewhere in the hills she'd be able to lose the men determined to steal Marron. Unfortunately, climbing the closest hill would have slowed them down and made them an easy target, so Abby had to bring her horse closer to her pursuers to get to the gap between the hills. As they lost ground, the bullets started to fly again. One whizzed by so close to her cheek, she felt the wave of air it left behind as it hurtled past. After another tense two minutes, Marron pulled away again. As they skirted the nearest hill, there was a shout from somewhere above her.

"Abby, get through the gap and keep goin'!"

Not questioning the command, Abby urged Marron on, barely entering the gap before multiple guns opened up from higher on the hillside. Once she'd reached the other side she slowed Marron, bringing him to a complete halt a quarter mile from the far end of the gap between two hills.

The gunfire had stopped. She waited, listening, trying to make out any sounds beyond Marron's hard breathing and her own drumming heartbeat.

Another ten minutes crawled by in silence. She'd dismounted and was giving her horse a drink from a wide-topped tin cup she kept just for that purpose, when three riders emerged from the gap and trotted in her direction.

As they got closer, she smiled and waved. "Hello, Mitch. How are you, Jake?"

The two men returned her smile and nodded their heads in greeting, but continued to ride past her.

"Make sure those cows weren't spooked by the shootin'," George Cowan said, stopping his own mount in front of Abby. He leaned forward and frowned at her. With hair more gray than brown, a full beard and skin turned permanently tan by the sun, he looked every inch like a ranch foreman. A very annoyed ranch foreman.

Abby bit her lower lip and gazed up at him. "Good afternoon, George."

He grunted and pointed a finger at her. "I suppose you had a good reason for not coming with the supply train?"

"I was unavoidably delayed," Abby said.

"You're supposed to stay with the supply wagon."

Abby shrugged. "Marron could have outrun those men, George. No harm would have come of it. But I do thank you for your help."

"Scarin' a few years off my life is harm enough considerin' I don't have as many of those left as you do," George said. He shook his head and scowled at her.

"I wish you'd stay where you're put, Doctor Abby."

August 1854
San Francisco, California

Chapter One

Charles Jamison flopped onto the overstuffed chair. He managed a smile for Alice as she arranged a tray of coffee, tea and small cookies on the side table. It looked inviting, but right at the moment he would have preferred a shot of the whiskey from the decanter sitting next to the tea service. To his dead mother's credit, his polite Southern upbringing kept his eyes from straying in that direction.

He'd wait to pour a drink until John made an appearance and Alice left the room. His good friend was meeting with a man Charles hoped was the solution to the rash of robberies targeting the patrons of his business.

The young, rowdy city of San Francisco was in dire need of better law enforcement. Charles hoped that need was about to be met.

Once California had gained its statehood and entrance to the Union three years before, thanks largely to the discovery of gold at Sutter Creek, the federal government had created the newly formed Northern California Judicial District. The newest district may have been dripping in gold dust from the mountains to the east, but it also had an exploding population along with a growing criminal problem, and still no marshal assigned to it. Rumor had it that President Pierce was set on appointing one sometime this year, but so far that had only been a rumor. Until now. And the reason was sitting in John's office.

"Do you think you'll be wanting anything else? I need to get the rest of the house clean and the meat prepared for dinner." Tall and thin, Alice stood ramrod straight with her hands clasped in front of her, and an unblinking stare directed at Charles.

"I don't believe so, Alice. Thank you." Charles tried his most charming smile. "How long has John been in with Mr. McKenzie?"

"Marshal McKenzie," Alice corrected with a slight rise in her voice. "Almost an hour, Mr. Jamison."

He shook his head at her. "After two years of an acquaintance, I don't suppose you could call me Charles?"

"It would not be proper, Mr. Jamison," Alice said.

"I see." Charles smiled but did a mental roll of his eyes.

Alice was certainly on a first name basis with John's wife, Beth, as well as with his own wife, Lillian, and even with Lillian's cousin, Abby, and her two good friends, Maggie and Rayne. But every male the housekeeper spoke to, no matter how long she'd known him, only merited a more formal address. That peculiar rule of hers included John, her employer.

Running a distracted hand through his thick dark hair, Charles shot another glance toward the open parlor door. He wondered how much longer before John and Marshal McKenzie would be finished talking.

He wanted to get back to *The Crimson Rose* and Lillian. His wife hadn't felt well that morning, even though she'd done her best to hide her illness from him. Of course such a small inconvenience wouldn't keep her from her planned get-together with her tightly knit, circle of friends. Not when her cousin had just returned from visiting Rayne and would have a full report on the expectant mother.

But the minute he'd concluded his business here, he intended to collect Lillian and put her back into bed no matter how much she protested. And he wasn't opposed to simply picking her up and carrying her upstairs so she could get the proper rest.

He never liked it when anything was wrong with Lillian.

"I believe Mr. Davis and the marshal have concluded their business," Alice announced, astonishing Charles with a tiny smile before she exited the room.

Charles rose to his feet when John and a tall man with broad shoulders came through the parlor door together. Charles nodded at his friend before he shifted his gaze and openly studied the US Marshal. Both John and his guest had the same hard, determined look in their eyes. Most likely because they were in the similar business of dealing with criminals. John was an investigator for his family's shipping business as well as a few other clients.

The marshal was an inch or so taller than John's six feet, but had the same light coloring and blue eyes, although the marshal's ran to a much deeper shade then John's.

Caden McKenzie was definitely a handsome man, if you overlooked the long gash running from the top of his cheekbone to his chin on the left side of his face. Charles doubted many looked past it.

Knife swipe, thin blade, he thought. His brown eyes shifted from the deep scar to Marshal McKenzie's steady stare.

"Charles, I'd like to introduce you to Marshal McKenzie." John turned and smiled at the marshal. "This is Charles Jamison, the good friend I was telling you about. He's one of the prominent businessmen in our city."

"Mr. Jamison." The marshal's deep voice was as calm as his gaze and gave very little away. He waited with an unnerving stillness while Charles closed the gap between them and held out his hand.

"Marshal."

As handshakes were exchanged, John nodded toward the divan and chairs clustered near the fireplace.

"Gentlemen, I suggest we make ourselves comfortable and discuss our mutual problem."

Charles looked over at John and then back at the marshal. "Mutual?"

Cade McKenzie gave an abrupt nod before following John across the room, settling into the matching overstuffed chair directly across from the one Charles had vacated to greet them. John reached up to the long, highly polished wooden mantel to retrieve a narrow box.

"Cheroot, gentlemen? My Southern friend here got me to switch over from the usual cigars. My wife was very grateful for the change, and I find it a necessary part of my life to make my wife happy." John shrugged when both men declined, but took one out and lit it from the hearth's fire with a long thin stick he plucked from a basket by the fireplace.

"Did your wife decorate this room?" The marshal hesitated for a long moment. "It's nice."

The question took Charles by surprise and John seemed at a sudden loss for words. Charles took a quick glance around the spacious parlor, decorated in quiet tones of blue and brown. It was clearly designed for comfort but had an understated elegance about it as well.

Lillian often maintained it was a perfect reflection of Beth.

"Yes, she did," John finally said. "I'll be sure to tell her you admired it."

Cade cleared his throat and wondered why he'd made such a ridiculous comment. He shouldn't have been noticing how comfortable and welcoming the room was, much less said what he was thinking out loud. The two men staring at him looked as if they thought he was crazy. And he couldn't blame them for that. It's not as though he'd never been in a civilized room. Lately he'd spent quite a bit of time in a proper home. At least as proper as he could make it.

Shaking the thought off, he slipped on his blank marshal face and turned to the dark-haired man, with his polite expression and Southern drawl, sitting across from him.

"I was just told we have a mutual problem. But I'm not sure how the gang I'm chasing affects you, Mr. Jamison?"

"Charles will suffice, Marshal McKenzie. As John said, I own a business in town and my wife owns a very special ranch a little more than a good day's ride from here. I'm also looking to buy more property outside town, and have hired someone to manage both the sale and then the property. He'll be traveling around the countryside quite a bit."

"So you think your wife's ranch is threatened by this gang, as well your other hired man?" Cade asked.

"And my business," Charles added. "When this gang comes into town, they target customers coming out of my gaming hall."

"Charles owns *The Crimson Rose*," John said.

Cade was silent. He'd been in *The Crimson Rose*. It was on the edge of the infamous Barbary Coast and its blocks of gambling halls, which grew more disreputable the further into The Coast a man roamed. But *The Crimson Rose* was the most elegant place Cade had ever seen, and from what he'd heard, it often catered to some very high stakes games.

"You're a gambler." Cade made it a flat statement as he continued to stare at the Southerner.

"An honest gambler, Marshal."

His dark, brown gaze didn't waver, and Cade had to give him a grudging respect for not backing down from a US Marshal. He hadn't met many gamblers with that kind of backbone. He gave another abrupt nod along with a slight smile.

"Cade. Cade will suffice."

He watched the gambler visibly relax. Cade waited a few moments longer before getting to his business.

"I'm after Ben Linder. He and his gang robbed a supply train from one of the rancheros near Los Angeles. A federal judge was riding along and was killed by one of Linder's men. We have good information that Linder and his gang headed north, to San Francisco, and the judge in this district has issued a warrant for their arrest. They could be the same men robbing your customers here in town."

"My informants tell me they are," John said. At the quick look from Cade, his shoulders rose and fell in a casual motion. "I told you I mostly work for my family's shipping business, but I have private clients as well. Charles is one of them. We have eyes and ears all over the city."

Cade nodded his understanding. "You said these same men are also attacking miners coming back from their claims?"

"Attacking and killing." John's mouth thinned into a straight line. "They've left witnesses. And have been spotted camping out in the hills far too close to the ranch."

"Your wife's ranch?" Cade turned to look at Charles.

"Lilian's ranch," Charles confirmed. "She has a ranch for the city's orphans. Gives them a place to grow up without worrying when they'll get something to eat, and she helps them get a start on their own when they're ready. Quite a few of them have stayed around and found work in the city."

The marshal smiled. It wasn't hard to guess who Davis and Jamison used as their eyes and ears about town.

It was also obvious by the tone in the man's voice how proud he was of his wife. And judging by the foolish look on his face when he said her name, it was clear he was deeply in love with the woman.

Cade had always been too busy for that sort of nonsense. First joining the army when he was twenty and itching to get away from home like most young men that age, and now ten years later he had the responsibility of raising his younger brother, and providing a home for his spinster cousin. He'd also seen what that kind of deep love for a woman could do to a man. It had killed his father, so Cade was content to do without it.

Putting his mind back to the business at hand, Cade frowned. He certainly couldn't have a gang of killers swarm down on a ranch full of orphans.

"I've contacted Sheriff Gorham here in the city," Cade stated. "He said he doesn't handle crimes outside town, and inside town all they've done is rob a few folks of their wallets who were too drunk to protest much about it at the time."

"Gorham is fine with me deputizing a few men and taking on Ben Linder. The man may turn and run even further north since his cousin, Frank, died in that last shootout. The Oregon territory doesn't have any US Marshals in it, so he may feel safer up there once he knows we're hunting him here. The best thing to do is stop him quick and have everyone stay out of his way until then." He looked over at Charles. "If you don't have enough hands to see to the job, you should send extra men to help guard the ranch. I can help you find a few."

"Since Marshal McKenzie is willing to help us, we should return the favor," John said turning to Charles. "The marshal needs a doctor. His brother is sick."

"Brother?" Charles asked.

"My younger half-brother," Cade clarified. "Geraldine heard that you know a doctor who might be able to help him." Cade rubbed a tired hand down the length of his scar. The rasp of stubble when he reached his chin reminded him he hadn't shaved that morning.

He'd spent the night in his younger brother's room after Jules had another of his mysterious breathing episodes. The boy had struggled for breath a good piece of the night, and when it had finally eased up enough for Jules to fall into a restless sleep, Cade hadn't dared to close his eyes. Over the last two years, since he'd taken on the task of raising his brother, Cade had lost count of the number of sleepless nights. Good thing for him he'd never slept much anyway.

If Jules was ever going to have a normal life, he needed help. So Cade looked the gambler in the eye and hoped Geraldine's information about this doctor was correct.

"Geraldine?" Charles asked.

"My cousin. She's also our cook and housekeeper. She did the same for my father too, before he took his own life."

After his years in the army, and what he'd seen in the war with Mexico, Cade never danced around the truth of things. It was a waste of time as far as he was concerned. And he didn't have any to waste. Jules needed help now. "The doctors in Chicago thought my brother would do better in a warmer climate, and he did for a while."

"And now he isn't?" Charles leaned forward, his hands on his knees, an unwavering gaze on Cade.

"It comes and goes. But recently it's been getting worse. He needs a doctor who can spend time with him, not just drop in every week or so to deliver the standard patter about growing boys and the benefits of sea air. Someone who's good with kids," Cade stated. "Jules is eleven, and he should be running around and getting into trouble, not spending most of his time in a bed."

"Your cousin's information was right. I know a doctor," Charles said slowly. He stopped there and looked down at his hands and then over at John.

Having caught the glance between the two men, the marshal's hands clenched around the arm of the chair and the muscles in his back went rigid as he braced himself for some excuse on why this doctor relative of Jamison's couldn't help Jules.

"She can help if anyone can. And as it turns out, catching that gang will help her."

"She?" Cade was expecting a refusal. He certainly didn't think he'd hear that the doc was a female.

"Doctor Abby. She has a practice in town and sees a number of children here. She also tends to the dozen or so children out at the ranch."

Cade blinked, still trying to adjust to a female doctor. He'd heard of them, but always had a vague idea they were all back East somewhere.

John walked over and sat on the divan. "She's an excellent doctor, Cade. She didn't go to a medical school, of course, but took her training under one of her father's closest friends. I understand he was a brilliant physician. There isn't much Doctor Abby doesn't know about medicine. Especially kids. And she reads up on it all the time. You can trust her with your brother."

Blowing out a breath, Cade sat back in his chair. His hand came up to touch his scar as he thought it over. He didn't know how Jules would react to a female doctor. Hell, he wasn't even sure how he felt about it.

"I assume all the doctors your brother had in Chicago were men?" Charles asked. At Cade's nod, the gambler smiled. "Then maybe you should try something different."

Cade turned that over in his mind for a long moment until he remembered something else Charles had mentioned.

"Why would catching the Linder gang help this doctor?"

His eyebrows shot up when John and Charles let out a groan in unison.

"She travels out to the ranch," John said.

Cade still didn't see the problem. Charles had already stated the doctor took care of the kids at the ranch.

"And across other parts of the countryside as well," Charles said, breaking into his thoughts. "We've both tried to arrange protection for her, and it's not a problem when the trips are planned."

"But she just up and goes whenever she gets word she's needed somewhere," John finished. "Next thing we know, we have to send men chasing after her."

Cade let out a snort and shook his head. "Have you told her how dangerous that is?"

Charles shot him a *you-must-be-joking* glare while John rolled his eyes.

"Sounds like she might know a lot about healing but lacks common sense." Cade smiled when Charles covered his eyes with one hand. "Find her a husband to take her off your hands. Let him figure out a way to protect her."

"I'm thinking my new ranch manager might fit that bill, and hopefully before I'm forced to send her back to her home to Connecticut just so we can all get a good night's sleep. But my wife would object, since the doctor is also her cousin. So I'd appreciate it if you'd catch Linder and his murdering band of thieves, and spare me one less worry," Charles said. "I have my hands full at *The Crimson Rose* and at home, plus the household where my sister and niece live."

John laughed. "Ammie and your sister, Charlotte, are Cook's problem most of the time, not yours."

Cade's interest was caught. "Cook? The cook is responsible for protecting your sister's household?"

"Cook is his name as well as occupation, although he's also the nanny and housekeeper when necessary."

"He?" Cade couldn't keep his mouth from dropping open. The little girl's nanny was a *he*?

"That's right. Things are done a bit different out West."

When Jamison broke into a grin, Cade rolled his eyes. The man was pulling his leg.

This cook person wasn't a male, and he'd bet the doctor wasn't female either. Unwilling to waste any more time on trivial matters, Cade nodded his understanding.

"Where can I find Dr. Abby?"

"I'll write down the directions for you. She's practicing with Dr. Melton, and the two of them cover each other's patients when the need arises."

"I appreciate it. I'll pay them a visit and see what I think." Cade ignored the reference to the "she". Jamison apparently didn't know when a joke was done.

Chapter Two

"When did you get back?" Maggie Dolan's green eyes radiated a warm welcome that Abby would never take for granted. She returned the smile before her gaze settled on the infant in Maggie's arms.

Just three months old, little Anna was perfect. With a distinct reddish cast in her baby-fine hair, she looked to be the spitting image of her Irish mother, with more than a hint of her proud papa in her hazel eyes.

"It looks as if she's grown another inch since I last saw her," Abby said. She set the peach pie she was carrying on the large table in the center of the kitchen and reached for the infant. Maggie carefully placed the squirming child into her arms.

"She's been a bit unsettled at night," Maggie said, peering into her daughter's face. "Not sure why this little one is havin' trouble sleepin'."

Doctor Abagail Metler shifted the baby in her arms before giving her a gentle bounce. She looked up when the other two women in the room crowded around her.

Her cousin Lillian, whom Abby was certain was the most stunning woman in the world with her platinum blond hair and flawless complexion, leaned over and traced a slim, gentle finger down Anna's tiny arm.

"She's beautiful," Lillian said before stretching over the baby and placing a kiss on Abby's cheek. "Welcome back."

Beth Davis placed a hand on Abby's shoulder and gave it a light squeeze. "We're so glad you're back, Abby. We want to hear all about Rayne and how she's doing."

Abby nodded and handed the baby to her mother. "Maggie, are you still giving Anna just milk?"

Her friend's eyes opened in surprise. "Just milk, you're sayin'? Because she demands enough of that. Has me up at all hours to feed her, she does."

Abby's blue eyes sparkled from behind wire-rimmed glasses. She tilted her head to one side. Long strands of hair, shot through with the entire palette of dark and light browns, instantly escaped the loose coil at the base of her neck as another hairpin popped loose and fell to the floor.

With a resigned sigh, Abby started to gather the pins up and stick them back into place.

"Maggie, didn't you bring Anna into my office three weeks ago?"

Maggie's eyebrows drew together, and Abby could almost see her mentally counting backwards before nodding her agreement.

"It was before you went to visit Rayne, so I'm thinkin' it was a good three weeks past."

"I thought so," Abby said. "Anna may have your coloring and temper, Maggie, but she most definitely shows signs of having a good piece of her father's height. I'd guess she's grown at least an inch and gained some weight since I last saw her. I think you should start feeding her mashed-up fruit, maybe some potatoes or yams. See if that will help her settle down better at night."

Maggie's eyes opened wide as she stared at her daughter. "As tall as that? Luke said everyone in his family was tall. All the Saint's know my Ian has some good height to him. And Luke, too. I didn't think he meant his sisters as well."

Abby gave the baby one last pat. "How is your brother-in-law?" She turned her head to glance at Lillian. "Is he still looking for ranch land for you and Charles?"

"Yes, he is. He's found a few good prospects but our lawyer friend here," Lillian gestured at Beth, "decided they wouldn't do, so he's still looking."

"The owners were absent. Most likely gone to the gold fields. They'd have to be found and asked if they're willing to sell their land," Beth said as she settled herself on one of the tall stools around the kitchen table. "Charles didn't want the complication."

The women were gathered in Lillian's spacious house with an elegant parlor they rarely made use of when it was just the four of them. Five, when Rayne came into town. They preferred the cozy atmosphere in the oversized kitchen. It suited them much better.

"Luke's happy to be lookin' since he'll be managin' the ranch. I'm sure you'll be hearin' about it at the supper get-together we'll be plannin'."

"Not to mention my husband's obvious hints about how Luke should settle down with a wife. Someone to keep him company during the lonely evening hours on the ranch." Lillian grinned at Abby.

"And don't forget how he's given Luke strict instructions to find a place located so anyone who happened to be living on the ranch could easily visit all the neighbors, and make the trip in no more than a day back into the city, if she had a mind to." Beth sent the doctor a broad wink.

"And he's a nice lookin' man. Tall, strong. More than able to take care of his own." Maggie laughed. "He is me husband's brother, so I'm thinkin' I should point out *his* good traits, instead of the ranch he'll be buyin'."

Lillian shook her head, sending her moonlit curls dancing around her shoulders. "Not my husband's usual subtle approach."

"I haven't heard Luke objecting. He usually just winks at Abby whenever Charles starts listing his finer qualities," Beth said.

"He doesn't object because he knows Abby isn't seriously considerin' it. If he thought she was, he'd be makin' himself scarce enough," Maggie declared.

Beth laughed. "I'd say our Doctor Abby isn't considering it at all, much less seriously."

Abby let the conversation swirl around her. She was content to listen to the voices teasing her, grateful these women considered her part of their family. Finding her cousin Lillian, after so many years believing she was dead, had not only been the biggest surprise in her life, but a precious gift as well.

Once the mystery of Lillian's disappearance as a young girl was solved, Abby was thrilled to stay permanently in San Francisco and open her medical practice where she felt her services were so desperately needed.

Her mother had chosen to return to Connecticut along with her conniving husband, Abby's stepfather. Frances Lathrope Metler Winston had never understood her daughter's desire to become a doctor, much less devote a good part of her time to the less fortunate. So it was no surprise when the Eastern matron took the steamer home once her long-lost niece, Lillian, was found, barely arguing with her daughter's decision to stay in San Francisco. Abby doubted if she'd ever see her mother again.

In her more private moments, Abby still mourned the loss of even the thin bond she'd had with Frances Metler. But the new family she'd gained certainly kept her busy enough that those moments of sad reflection hadn't happened very often.

Over the last year she'd grown close to her cousin and her husband, Charles, along with his niece, Ammie, whom they were raising, as well as with Beth, Maggie, Rayne and their husbands. Every person in Lillian's extended family circle had accepted her into their homes and their hearts, and Abby, an only child who'd spent most of her time studying medicine under the tutelage of a good friend of her father's, now found herself thinking of these four women as sisters.

Despite all of Charles's hints, she didn't need or want a husband. And had no time in her busy day to look after one. She had everything and more she'd ever need in her life. And if her sisters and their husbands had their way, more than enough children would be coming along for her to take care of well into her old age.

With the miracle of a large family, a steadily growing list of patients, and work she truly loved, Abby was more than content. She was happy.

With the thought spreading warmth through her body, she took a stool next to Lillian's and lifted her cousin's wrist. Placing two fingers on the inside pulse, she smiled at Lillian's raised eyebrows.

"How are you feeling?"

"I feel fine, except for a little bit of sickness in the morning."

"Perfectly natural," Abby assured her.

Maggie shifted the now sleeping Anna in her arms and added her nod of agreement. "I told her the same and brought over a blend of tea to help."

"Maggie's advice is sound. Tea can help calm your stomach in the morning. And I'm sure Master Kwan can recommend an herb or two as well. I'll ask him the next time I'm running an errand in Little Canton," Abby said, referring to the part of the city where the Chinese immigrants had settled.

Her cousin laughed. "Do you think Master Kwan has something to keep Charles calm? I haven't even told him the good news yet and he's already fussing."

Abby's sky-blue eyes crinkled in amusement. "I'm sorry to tell you, but fussing husbands go with expectant mothers. Rayne is having much the same problem with Tremain. I've never seen a man hover over another person the way he is with Rayne. I think he's in danger of his wife shooting him."

"Well, I'm sorry to hear that," Lillian said. "Especially considering Tremain is Charles's brother and the two of them act so much alike."

"Between worrying about his wife and his cousin-in-law, Charles will be nothing but a bag of nerves by the time this baby makes his or her appearance," Beth said.

"He's wasting his time worrying about me," Abby declared. "I lead a very quiet life."

All three women stared at her with their eyes popping out of their heads. Abby looked back at them and frowned.

"Of course my life is quiet," Abby insisted.

"I spend the entire day seeing patients, and now in my free time I run errands for Paul, since he broke a bone in his foot," she said, referring to the older physician she shared space with to see their patients. "I don't have time to get into enough mischief to worry Charles."

Lillian crossed her arms in front of her and shook her head at her cousin. "Mischief wouldn't worry him. Almost getting yourself killed does."

"You got thrown from your horse comin' back from Lillian's ranch, and had to walk a good five miles back into town," Maggie stated.

"Then there were the men who chased you across the hills because they wanted your horse," Beth chimed in. "Scared Carrie half to death when George told her about seeing you racing across the countryside, being shot at."

"I didn't mean to scare them," Abby said. She really did feel bad about that. Carrie was a wonder to look after so many children on Lillian's ranch, and George was the sweetest man, when he wasn't aiming a shotgun at a stray mountain lion, or a couple of men determined to steal her horse.

"Well, you did," Beth flatly stated. "And all of us, too, plus our worry-prone husbands. Honestly, Abby. You can't just go riding off at the blink of an eye. You should take at least one of the stable hands with you."

Abby simply smiled. Danny and the newest hand, Little Jake, were very nice young men. But neither had been off the ranch long, and both were just over eighteen. That put them a good eight years behind her, so in her mind they were more like younger brothers or nephews, than "protection".

Besides, she'd never put either young man into a situation that she could take care of herself by simply outrunning the bad men, or animal, or whatever was a threat. Wasn't that the reason she had Marron, one of the prized stallions from Rayne's ranch? Abby was sure there wasn't a horse in the entire country that could outrun Marron. Not to mention the hours and hours Rayne spent working with her new doctor friend to sharpen her riding skills. The rancher's daughter always staunchly maintained if you only had one skill to take out into the open country, it was expert riding.

"... especially with this new gang of outlaws running about the country between here and the ranch."

"Excuse me?" Abby pushed at her glasses and looked over at Lillian. "What new gang?"

"The one that's robbed people all over the city. Including a fair number of patrons from *The Crimson Rose*," her cousin said. "Weren't you listening to the men talk about them when we all got together before you left for Rayne's ranch?"

"The same bunch John's been chasing for the last three months." Beth's mouth turned down at the corners. "I hate it when he chases killers."

"Abby." Maggie's green eyes went a shade darker as she looked at her friend. "We all know how you feel about rushin' off to see any of your patients out at the ranch, or anywhere else, for that matter. But you can't keep goin' alone. If you won't do it for your own safety, then think of savin' the sanity of my Ian, Beth's John, and Charles. Tremain, too. When the men are together, they spend a fair amount of time talkin' about how to keep you safe."

"That's true," Lillian said. "We worry about you, Abby. And there's no use shaking your head about it. That's what families do."

"It's just common sense," Beth said, leaning forward as she fixed her gaze on Abby. "And with this new threat, you're tempting fate to go off by yourself whenever you get word that someone needs help."

"I have to help, Beth. I took an oath." Abby's tone was quiet but firm. She took her duties as a doctor very seriously. Just as her mentor back in Connecticut had taught her. For Abby, there was no other way.

"I've read that oath, Abagail Metler. It didn't say a word about havin' to rush off the instant a patient sends for you. Takin' the extra hour or so to be sure a few strong men go with you isn't violatin' your oath." Maggie wrinkled her nose and narrowed her eyes, a sure sign she wasn't going to give up the argument.

"And men who can shoot straight," Beth said. When Abby frowned at her, she simply shrugged. "It's serious enough that John and Charles are seeing a US Marshal this morning."

She nodded at the surprised gasps around the table. "He's hoping Marshal McKenzie will see this as a federal matter and be willing to help out with this gang."

"Abby, you simply have to be more cautious," Lillian insisted.

Seeing the concerned faces around the table, Abby slowly nodded. "I'll do my best."

When no one said a word but just continued to stare, she indulged in a rare dramatic gesture and placed one hand over her heart. "I promise to be extra careful. I do not want anything to do with men who kill."

Chapter Three

Cade paused by the low, iron gate surrounding the solid-looking house that was tucked along the edge of the city's business district. Only a few blocks from the bay, the squared off facade had wide stone steps leading up to a front door that was flanked on either side by large windows. A neatly painted sign, with white letters on a black background, showed *Dr. P. Melton.*

The look of the place was promising, except Dr. Abby's name was missing from the sign. Still, the address was right so Cade shrugged it aside, pushed open the gate, and strode up the path. Since there was no knocker, only a small discreet notice hanging from the handle stating the doctor was in, Cade barely hesitated on the front steps before walking into the house. He shut the door behind him without turning his back on the room, a habit from his time in the army that also served him well as a marshal.

He'd stepped directly into a large parlor, with several ladder-backed chairs lining three of the walls. Cade's glance rapidly quartered the room. Nodding politely at the two women who'd looked up at his entrance before immediately looking away, he sized up the only other male occupying a chair. Dressed in a tweed suit and white shirt with a very stiff collar, the short, thinly built man looked as if he belonged behind a desk in some bank. Which is where he apparently left his manners since his eyes were riveted on Cade's scar.

Used to being gaped at, and in truth much worse reactions, Cade ignored him. He moved out of the door way and to one side, where he had a clear view of the street through the large window. Keeping the wall at his back, he braced his legs apart and crossed his arms over his wide chest, not bothering to remove his broad-brimmed hat. He'd been as polite as he was going to be. Resigned to a long wait, he turned his attention to watching the people and carriages passing by on the street. It was a good ten minutes before the door at the back of the room finally opened and two, well-dressed men emerged. The older man leaned heavily on a cane.

"You make sure you take that cough medicine every morning and every night. I don't want to make a house call in the middle of the night because you're wheezing yourself into an early grave."

"Charming thought, doctor," the taller man said, slipping the bottle into his coat pocket.

"True, nevertheless. My best wishes to your lovely wife." With a short wave, the doctor dismissed his patient and turned to survey the people in his waiting room. His bushy eyebrows, which were a direct contrast to the very thin hair on his head, lowered into a scowl as his gaze settled on Cade. "If you're a new patient, I'm afraid you'll be waiting awhile. You're welcome to come back in an hour or so unless you have some sort of emergency?"

Cade shook his head. "No emergency. I came to talk to Dr. Abby. Is that you?"

Those same bushy eyebrows shot up as one of the female patients let out a giggle, quickly covered by a discreet cough. Cade felt every eye in the room on him but he didn't move a muscle, or take his gaze off the doctor.

The man cleared his throat and leaned both hands on his cane. "I'm Dr. Melton. Maybe we should step inside my office." He looked around the room as he thumped his cane once on the solid, wood floor. "I'll only be a few minutes. I should remind you that I don't look kindly on gossip, and I'm the only doctor in town who isn't an outright fraud, besides Doctor Abby, of course, so it would be best to stay in my good graces."

Without another word, he went through the back door. Cade strode after the doctor who continued to limp down a short hallway, turning into a room at the far end. The doctor gestured toward a simple, wooden chair. Cade sat while Dr. Melton slowly made his way around a large desk. He stood behind it, leaning on his cane as he studied the tall, intimidating man dwarfing his visitor chair.

"Tell me why you're looking for Dr. Abby? You aren't a patient."

"Why would you say that?" Cade asked.

"I'm familiar with all our patient's and I don't know you, sir. Who are you?"

"I'm Cade McKenzie. Marshal McKenzie."

The doctor snorted. "You aren't going to tell me Doctor Abby is in trouble with the law, are you? Because that would be impossible."

The marshal's dark-blue stare sharpened as he leaned back into his chair. "Why would you say that?"

"Not much on answering questions, are you, young man? And you may as well put that stare away. It might work on most, but I've been practicing medicine longer than you've been alive. I've seen enough in those years that you don't scare me one bit. Having said that, you may as well tell me why you want to see Doctor Abby?

Cade's mouth curled into a smile at the direct challenge he saw in the doctor's eyes. The older man wanted his answers, and other than being conditioned to keep things to himself, Cade had no reason not to oblige him. With a shrug, he relaxed his shoulders and removed his hat, setting it onto his bent knees. He ran a hand across his scar.

"Dr. Abby came recommended by Charles Jamison and John Davis."

"Not surprised," the man standing across the desk said. "Charles and the doctor are related."

"So I heard."

"Cousins, by marriage," Dr. Melton confirmed. "And you still haven't answered my question. Why do you want to see the doctor? You seem healthy enough."

32

"I have a younger brother who's got a breathing ailment that won't go away. His doctor back in Chicago couldn't help him."

"And you think Doctor Abby can?"

"Hoping," Cade corrected. "Jules is only eleven. He deserves a chance to live out a normal life, and not one confined to a bed."

"Odds are in your brother's favor. If anyone can help him, Doctor Abby can. Most brilliant physician I've ever had the pleasure of knowing." The older man nodded. "Can the boy come here, or would a visit to your home be better?"

A small wave of relief moved through Cade. Help from a real doctor rather than relying on Geraldine's homemade remedies was a big weight off his mind. Naturally he wasn't at all convinced this supposedly brilliant doctor could cure Jules. They'd already seen several of the best doctors in Chicago. But Cade had to do something. He hated not being able to help his brother.

He took out a card with his address written on it. "Here's where we live. The doctor can come any time."

"Doctor Abby's been out of town, but should be back in the office to see patients tomorrow. I'll make sure to deliver your message."

"I appreciate it."

With nothing more to say, Cade picked up his hat and rose to his feet in one, fluid motion. After a brief nod to the doctor, who continued to study him, Cade turned on his heel and left the office. He made his way through the outer room, not even sparing a glance at any of the occupants.

He'd barely stepped outside before he collided with another, much smaller body. Cade dropped his hat as his hands instinctively shot out and closed around the upper arms of a woman, who was perilously close to tumbling backwards down the steps. The package she'd been holding went flying through the air, along with her bonnet, when she grabbed onto his arms. Several hairpins bounced against his chest as long strands of soft hair unraveled from the coil at the back of her neck and slipped over his hands.

"Good heavens," a purely feminine voice said.

Cade looked down just as the softest blue eyes he'd ever seen peered up at him. A delicate hand reached out to shove a mass of hair back over one shoulder and her eyes narrowed into a tiny squint as she continued to stare up at him through the wire-rimmed spectacles perched at an odd angle on her nose. His gaze passed slowly over her face, taking in every detail of full lips and a complexion the color of a rich cream with a hint of honey. He moved on to the thick tangle of hair with a varied spread of many shades of brown, falling in long, lazy curls that almost reached to her waist.

"Are you all right?"

The quiet voice surprised him, and the sensual feel of her hair gliding over the back of his hand sent electric shimmers up his arm. Not sure he liked either sensation, Cade's jaw hardened enough to create a slight tic in his cheek.

"I'm fine." The hard rasp in his voice had him clenching his teeth together even harder.

"Please, take the time you need to catch your balance."

When she smiled at him, Cade instantly let go of her.

"My balance is just fine, ma'am." He gave his head a slight shake and looked away for several moments, forcing his senses back from the strange place he didn't recognize. When he felt in control again, he glanced back at her.

She was still standing close, her gaze on his face, but her hands were busy putting her hair back into a rather lopsided coil. When she twisted to look at the ground, Cade sighed and knelt to pick up several hairpins. Straightening back to his full height, he held out his hand while she plucked up the pins one at a time and she secured her hair back into place.

Cade silently admitted he was sorry to see that. The image of her standing there, looking up at him with her hair tumbling all around her would be a picture he'd keep in his mind a long time.

"I'm Dr. Metler. And you are?"

By the time Cade managed to squash the image and register she was introducing herself, he only had a vague impression of her name, but it sounded as if she said she was Dr. Melton. And that made no sense, since he'd just met the man.

"I'm Cade McKenzie. And I apologize," Cade finally got out. "I shouldn't have come through the door so fast."

"No harm done. Except to Paul's dinner, I'm afraid."

Cade followed the direction of her gaze to the whole chicken and slices of carrot spread along the walkway behind her.

"Paul?"

"Dr. Melton. He asked me to bring his dinner on my way home."

Oddly disappointed, he realized she must have introduced herself as Dr. Melton's wife. Who else would be bringing the man dinner? Cade immediately took a half step to the side, putting as much distance between them as the small stoop would allow.

"I'd be happy to purchase another meal to replace this one," he offered.

"No need. There's more where that came from."

Realizing how much he wished she wasn't married to the doctor, and not liking that sudden, intense feeling either, Cade resorted to his usual behavior. He raised a polite hand to the brim of his hat and gave a short, quick nod before stepping around her and taking the steps two at a time. He glanced back after he was safely out past the iron gate. She was gone.

He stared at the closed door to the house until he felt foolish. Taking a deep breath, he tucked his hands into the pockets of the long rain slicker he always wore, and continued toward the center of town.

***

Several hours later, having finished his business at the bank, followed by a short drop-in on Sheriff Gorham, Cade strode across the porch and made his way into the house he'd leased for his small, tight-knit family. He smiled at his cousin Geraldine when she came bustling out of the kitchen, wiping her hands on her apron.

"Dina," he said, using the nickname he'd called her his entire life. "How's Jules doing?"

Closer to his mother's age than his own, Geraldine McKenzie was short, round and as practical a woman as Cade had ever met. He always thought she'd make some man a fine wife, but she preferred managing the household of his father and Jules. Cade hadn't objected at all when she'd assumed she'd stay on and continue to take care of his younger brother after his father chose to be with his beloved wife, rather than stay around for his young son. In fact, Cade was relieved beyond words to have Geraldine running his house.

Dina crossed the foyer and held out her hand for his hat and slicker. "You wash up, and then I'll give you a full report on Jules."

Having learned long ago not to argue with her, Cade did as he was told, making his way to the kitchen in the back of the house and the clean bucket of water Dina always kept by the sink. He made short work of washing the dust off his hands and face before returning to the front parlor. Dina handed him a sparkling, crystal glass filled half-way with his favorite whiskey.

Cade sank into one of the chairs and took a sip before looking over at his cousin, one eyebrow raised in a silent question.

"He's done better today. Just before you came in I managed to coax him into having a bite of bread to help settle his stomach. He fell asleep straight away, and hopefully will stay asleep for the rest of the night." Dina paused as she looked at him, biting her lip.

"I had some luck with John Davis," Cade said.

"You did?" Dina scurried over to a chair next to his and plopped down, barely taking a moment to smooth her skirts out. "Did he know the doctor I heard about?"

Nodding, Cade took another sip of his brandy. "Had a relative of this doctor, a Charles Jamison, come meet me this morning. After we got through discussing the Linder gang, we talked about the doctor. His name is Dr. Abby. He'll be back in town tomorrow and should be coming by the house in a day or so."

"Thank the Lord," Dina said, a smile spanning her entire face. "He sees a lot of children?"

"According to Davis and Jamison, he spends quite a bit of time with children. And according to Dr. Melton, he's brilliant," Cade said.

"Well, that certainly remains to be seen," Dina declared. "But I'll be keeping an eye out for him."

Chapter Four

Cade stirred in the chair he'd shoved next to his brother's bed so he could prop his stockinged feet on the end of it. Dina's hope that Jules would have a peaceful night's sleep wasn't to be, and Cade spent more long hours trying to keep the restless boy comfortable.

The mysterious rash that appeared in gashes on Jules's back, torso and limbs didn't look as bad as it had on previous occasions. Or maybe it was just his own wishful thinking, Cade mused, scrubbing a hand across his scar. He worried about how long Jules could continue to fend off whatever kept attacking his body.

He turned at the soft knock on the door. It was partially open and Dina's head peered around the edge. She cast a quick look to the bed's occupant before gesturing for Cade to come out into the hallway.

With a slight grimace, Cade rose and did a fast stretch, trying to loosen up the kink that had settled into his back. He laid a hand on the coverlet and leaned over enough to check and be sure Jules was still sleeping. Satisfied his brother was finally getting some real rest, Cade quietly tiptoed out of the room. Because he intended to sit with Jules for another hour, he didn't bother to collect his boots before joining his cousin in the hallway.

Since he'd left the bedroom door open, Cade lowered his voice to a hoarse whisper. "What do you need, Dina?"

The normally cheerful woman stood with pursed lips and her arms crossed over her bosom. Her long bed coat didn't quite cover the length of her nightgown, or the thick socks on her feet. A braid, threaded through with dark brown and gray hair, straggled down her back, and her eyes narrowed as she looked up at him.

"There's a woman downstairs to see you."

Cade couldn't have been more surprised if she'd said there was a mule in the parlor. He glanced toward the window at the end of the hallway and frowned. Judging by the weak light outside, he guessed it was only a couple of hours past dawn. Too early for a social visit, even if he knew someone to be socializing with. And given his line of work, he didn't get too many business calls from women.

"Who is it?" He thought it was a reasonable question, but Dina's eyes narrowed even further into tiny slits.

"I wouldn't know. But she claims you sent for her." Dina started tapping her foot. "At this hour of the night."

"The sun is up, Dina," Cade pointed out.

"It's too early for decent folks to be calling," Dina insisted. "I left her on the front porch."

When Cade didn't move, she reached out and poked him in the chest. "Well? Aren't you going to go say hello to your woman friend?"

The tone of her voice made it very clear just what kind of "friend" Dina thought had come looking for him.

"When I want female companionship, I don't bring her to the house."

"Cade McKenzie, have your manners completely deserted you?" Dina put her hands on her hips and stamped her foot hard enough to make the floorboards creak in protest.

Cade took a deep breath and touched his hand to his cheek. Dina was right. He shouldn't have said such an outrageous thing to any woman, much less his unmarried cousin. He must be more tired than he realized.

"I'm sorry. It's been a long night. I'm assuming the lady is looking for Marshal McKenzie and has a problem."

"She didn't ask for *Marshal* McKenzie, she asked for *Cade* McKenzie," Dina said, but her hands came off her hips and she didn't sound quite as angry. "Maybe I should come with you. If she *is* looking for the marshal, she might need something warm to drink."

39

"I'd appreciate it. *I* could certainly use it."

He rubbed his eyes, tiptoed back into the bedroom and retrieved his boots, then headed toward the stairs with Dina following at a slower pace. His cousin was still negotiating the steps when Cade, his boots back on his feet, strode across the small foyer and opened the front door.

"I'm sorry to keep you waiting Mrs…" He trailed off mid-sentence and gaped at the woman standing on his front porch.

"Metler," Abby said, offering a smile. "Actually, it's Dr. Metler."

"His wife." Cade stated, unable to stop staring at her.

Confused, Abby blinked several times. "Whose wife?"

"The doctor's."

Deciding the handsome man she'd almost run over on her office steps, and who'd popped into her mind at odd moments ever since, was clearly a bit addled, Abby tried a smile on the woman peeking around him. The same one who'd answered the door and then practically shut it in her face. Abby would have left if she hadn't believed there was a sick child in the house. But given their rather peculiar behavior, now she wasn't so sure staying was a good idea. It also seemed quite possible there wasn't a child here at all. Nevertheless, as she'd made the trip out so early in the morning, she might as well find out why they needed a doctor.

"I'm Dr. Abagail Metler," she tried again, keeping her smile aimed at the short woman who'd first greeted her. "Are you Mrs. McKenzie?"

"It's Miss McKenzie." The woman frowned for a moment. "Did you say your name is Abagail?"

Abby nodded. "I did." Before she could blink, the woman leaped out from behind the much larger man, almost knocking him off his feet.

"Come in, please come in. I'm so sorry to have left you out on the porch, but I didn't realize who you were."

40

Before she knew it, Abby's arm was firmly latched onto and she was being pulled past the completely silent man and into a foyer lit with a single candle on a side table.

"You come right into this parlor, now, and get comfortable. I'm going to make us tea so we can have a nice talk. Unless you prefer coffee? I'm Geraldine, by the way."

The woman kept up a stream of chatter as Abby found herself herded along into a homey room at the front of the house, and all but pushed onto the divan. She set her medical bag on the floor and continued to smile at Geraldine as the woman scurried around the room lighting candles.

A calm approach to this whole strange situation seemed to be her best course of action.

"I do prefer coffee, thank you. How is our patient?" Abby asked, thinking she should first confirm if there really was a patient here.

Geraldine bit her lip and looked over at Cade. "He didn't do very well last night."

Abby nodded then turned her attention to the still silent man. She adjusted her spectacles and hoped she could coax him into making sense. "Are you the patient? I understood I was asked to examine a young boy."

"No, I'm not the patient." Cade crossed his arms over his chest and braced his legs apart.

"You just find those manners you lost somewhere, Cade McKenzie," Geraldine said. "She's come to help Jules. Didn't you hear her? This is Abagail Metler. Doctor Abby."

When Cade's jaw dropped open, Abby simply gave him an angelic smile and a shrug before nodding at Geraldine.

"There's no need for an introduction. I told him my name the first time we met."

Geraldine's mouth formed into an "O" before her hands were once more on her hips and she glared at her cousin. "You didn't tell me you'd already met Doctor Abby."

"I didn't know I had," Cade said, his stare never leaving Abby's face.

"We very literally ran into each other on the steps outside my practice," Abby offered. "He seemed a little confused then, too."

"I am not confused," Cade snapped.

Geraldine's head shot around and she glared at him again. "Well, you're acting like the hind-end of a mule. Aunt Patricia would be very disappointed."

"Who's Aunt Patricia?" Abby asked, doing her best to contain the laughter threatening to bubble right out of her. Cade McKenzie was turning beet-red, and looked as if he wanted to strangle the woman.

"His mother," Geraldine said. "Now I'm going to get that coffee, and you," she pointed at her cousin, "stir up the fire so the doctor can get warm while we tell her about Jules."

After Geraldine marched out of the room, Abby blinked at Cade who still hadn't moved.

"And who is Jules?"

Cade stayed silent for a long moment before finally rubbing a hand across his scar. The gesture had Abby relaxing a bit.

"Jules is my brother. Your patient, or at least your potential patient." Cade moved past her to squat in front of the fireplace. He grabbed a metal poker and began stirring up the banked embers. When a small flame leaped out of the ashes, he reached for a log from the stack on the side and carefully placed it on top. Standing, he turned to face Abby.

"Why don't we start over? I'm Cade McKenzie. Marshal Cade McKenzie. And I take it you go by the name Doctor Abby, and are the cousin-in-law to Charles Jamison?"

Abby nodded and frowned as she recalled the conversation with her friends. "Marshal McKenzie? The man who's chasing the Linder gang?"

He nodded his head. "We'll get to that. Are you married to Dr. Melton?"

Taken aback, Abby's eyes widened as she stared up at him. "Of course not. We're partners and share a friendship, nothing more. Why would you think so?"

"Because you introduced yourself with the name of Melton, called him Paul and were bringing dinner to his place of business. All the things a wife does."

Not sure if he actually believed that's what she'd said when they'd first met, Abby was back to wondering if the marshal wasn't addled after all.

"You're just con..." At Cade's frown, she changed directions. "... not remembering correctly." She kept her voice soft and gentle. "I said *Metler*, not Melton. I told you I was Dr. Metler. And I was bringing Paul dinner because he's not getting around as well as he usually does." She paused for a moment, not surprised when the man staring at her remained silent. "Dr. Melton is using a cane. Remember?"

"I'm not confused and my memory is just fine, Doctor." Cade's voice held a noticeable snap. "I guess I didn't hear the name right the first time you said it."

"All right," Abby agreed. That really did sound reasonable enough. "Since we've cleared that up, is Geraldine a relation of yours? She said her name was McKenzie."

"My cousin," Cade said. "How did you know I came to capture the Linder gang?"

"Beth said so."

"And who is Beth?" Cade asked.

"I don't suppose if I simply said a good friend of mine you'd be happy with that answer?" Abby smiled when Cade shook his head. "Beth Davis."

"Any relation to John Davis?" Cade asked.

"Yes, she's his wife." Abby's smile grew wider. With the name confusion cleared up, the marshal didn't seem the least bit addled. Which made her feel better about him carrying a gun.

Geraldine bustled back into the room, balancing a large tray with cups and saucers. Sometime during her absence she'd changed out of her coat and nightgown and into a simple skirt and blouse, with a crisp white apron tied around her middle.

"It will take a few more minutes for the water to boil. Have you two managed to come to an understanding?"

"Not yet," Cade said without taking his eyes off Abby. "But we're getting to it."

Abby rolled her eyes at him before turning to Geraldine. "Tell me about Jules."

"He's a fine boy. Very handsome. And smart as a whip, too. Just like his father and brother."

"Dina," Cade interrupted. Abby noticed he was back to his arms being crossed over his chest. "I think the doctor wants to hear what's wrong with him."

"I'm just telling her a bit about Jules, is all. I'm sure it's important to know everything about her patient."

Cade snorted, but when Abby gave her an encouraging nod, Geraldine launched into a long description of the many finer points of her youngest cousin. After a few minutes it dawned on Abby that Geraldine desperately wanted her to like Jules. Hoping to ease the woman's worry, Abby reached for her bag and stood.

"I'd be happy to help Jules any way I can. May I see him now?"

"Of course, of course," Geraldine said. "Cade can take your bag up for you."

Abby shook her head at Cade when he started to reach for it. She turned away slightly and pulled it in closer to her. She never let anyone touch her medical bag. "No need. I've toted it across most of the countryside, so I'm comfortable carrying it myself."

"Something else we haven't come to an understanding about yet," Cade said, but he dropped his hand back to his side.

Abby's brow instantly furrowed. "Excuse me?"

"We'll talk about it later. Jules is upstairs." Cade gestured toward the parlor doors, politely waiting for the two women to precede him.

Well, Abby thought as she followed Geraldine up the steep staircase. *At least he found his manners.*

Chapter Five

Abby smiled at the boy sitting up against a mountain of pillows, trying to win her over with an adorable grin. A thick lock of blond hair fell in a gentle wave over his forehead, dipping over the same deep sea-blue eyes as his brother. It was no wonder Geraldine was happy to sing his praises. Even at eleven, Jules was a charmer. And a great deal friendlier than his older sibling, Abby thought.

She'd barely introduced herself before her patient began asking her a running litany of questions. Was she really a doctor? Had she ever cut anyone open? Did she like children? Did she own a horse? Abby patiently answered every question, biding her time until he finally wound down to a smiling silence. With so much hope reflected in his innocent gaze, how could she disappoint him? Somewhere there was an answer for what ailed Jules McKenzie, and she meant to find out what it was, and hopefully a cure as well.

"Jules, you talk more than a preacher on a Sunday. Are you ready to let the doctor have a say now?" Cade asked, softening his words by reaching out and ruffling his brother's hair.

Jules ducked away, but the grin stayed on his face. He nodded and shifted his gaze back to Abby.

"We do need to have a talk. Let's start with how you're feeling?" Abby picked up his wrist and put two fingers on his pulse, counting as she kept her eye on the pocket watch she'd placed on the bed.

"Lots better than I did last night. I couldn't breathe so well, but now I can." He took in a deep breath and blew it out again before grinning at her.

Used to patients trying to convince her there was nothing wrong with them, Abby smiled and nodded. "I can see you're fine."

"Cade had to sit with him last night, to be sure he kept breathing," Geraldine said. Abby was sure the older woman was going to be wringing her hands at any moment. "He's had these attacks for years, off and on. They're usually worse at night. Scares me half to death."

Abby looked at her and then at Cade, who dipped his head in agreement. When she glanced back at her patient, Jules had lost most of his bravado and was lying back against the pillows, his eyes downcast as he picked at a thread in the quilt covering his bed. A minute ago he'd been full of life, now he was as wilted as a week-old bouquet.

"I require privacy when I examine any of my patients." Abby addressed her remark to the two adults hovering behind her.

"But we're his family. He may need us," Geraldine protested.

"You can stay right outside in the hallway. It's close enough you'll be able to hear him call you," Abby said. She intended to stand firm on this point, and Geraldine must have realized the doctor meant what she said because she slowly began to back out of the room.

"You'll call if you need me, won't you Jules?" she asked just as she reached the doorway.

"Yes, Dina," Jules said. To Abby's ear, he already sounded more cheerful.

Once Geraldine disappeared into the hallway, Abby turned and raised an eyebrow at Cade. He crossed his arms over his chest and frowned.

"You didn't mean you wanted me to leave as well, did you?"

Abby tilted her head to one side. "Actually, I did."

"I need to hear what's going on," Cade replied, his boots staying firmly planted right where they were.

"I'll give you a full accounting once I've completed my exam. But not before, Marshal McKenzie."

The two stared at each other for a long minute before Cade finally relented.

"I'll be out in the hallway if you need me, Jules," Cade said, not taking his eyes off Abby.

"All right." Jules grinned at his brother and even added a jaunty wave.

"After the exam," Abby repeated. "We'll talk then."

Cade blew out a breath and touched a hand to his cheek before finally crossing the room in three long strides, closing the door behind him. Satisfied she'd have her patient's full attention without any interruptions, Abby sat on the edge of the bed.

"Now then, Jules. Tell me about last night."

***

A good hour later Abby emerged from the room. She wasn't surprised to find both Geraldine and Cade in the hallway. Geraldine was sitting on a plain wooden chair Abby hadn't noticed before, while Cade leaned against the wall next to the bedroom door. He straightened up when Abby appeared.

Geraldine pushed herself to her feet. "How is he?"

"He's fine," Abby reassured her. "He's resting. I think a nap will be good for him considering how poorly he slept last night."

"Of course, of course. Why don't we go to the parlor and I'll make us a pot of coffee." Dina turned and went down the hallway, heading for the front staircase.

Abby glanced over at Cade, who made a slight bow and held out one hand, palm up. "After you, Doctor Abby."

Smiling at how ridiculously formal he sounded, Abby inclined her head and lifted her skirt with one hand as she clutched her tapestry-covered medical bag in the other. She kept to a sedate walk, taking a secret pleasure in knowing how difficult it must be for the much bigger Cade McKenzie to adjust his long stride to her shorter one. But she didn't hear a peep of protest from the man, who followed her too closely to be quite proper. But she wasn't inclined to mention that breech of etiquette. Having him near gave her an odd sense of security. *But then, that shouldn't be a surprise. After all, he is a US Marshal. He's supposed to make a body feel safe,* Abby thought.

By the time they'd reached the parlor, Geraldine was walking along the back hall, carrying a tray with a pot and three cups and saucers. Cade intercepted her and took the tray out of her hands. That simple act sent a wiggle of warmth through Abby and had her mentally giving him higher marks for his manners. It seemed the man did have a few after all. And very gentlemanly ones, too.

Once they were settled with cups of hot coffee in their hands, Abby calmly smiled at the two people looking back at her so expectantly.

"Jules looked a bit underweight for his size, but not overly so for a boy who's growing so rapidly," she began, setting her cup aside. "Apart from a little raspiness in his breathing, and the welts on his back, he's reasonably healthy for all he's been through."

"Welts?" Cade asked quietly.

"It looks like a rash, but if you examine the area closely, it appears raised and in a longer shape. I would call them welts more than a rash."

Cade's fingers drummed on the arm of his chair. "Is that important? Whether it's a welt or a rash?"

"It could be," Abby said. "But let's talk about these attacks."

For the next half hour she asked questions, and they both answered with their own version of when and where Jules's breathing problem had happened. Abby listened carefully, arranging everything she heard in her mind. Her instincts kept drawing her in a single direction.

"Can you help him, Doctor Abby?"

Geraldine's simple question, along with the underlying plea in her voice, touched Abby's heart. She leaned over and placed her hand on top of one of Geraldine's and gave it a soft squeeze. "I'm going to do my very best. And there *is* something I want to try."

Both Cade and Geraldine sat up straighter, their gazes fixed on her face.

Abby nodded and looked directly at Geraldine. "For the next week, I only want him to eat broth and meat."

"Broth and meat?" Geraldine's forehead wrinkled and one hand came up to cover her mouth. "For every meal?"

"Yes. And a very particular broth, which I'll have sent over, along with someone who can write the recipe out for you."

"All right." Geraldine drew in a deep breath and managed a tiny smile. "Is there a special type of meat as well?"

"It needs to be fresh meat and not cured. And well cooked, with no seasonings." Abby smiled at the older woman's gasp. "He'll complain nothing tastes very good, but it's important to follow these instructions."

Geraldine gave a slow nod, her hands clasped so tightly in her lap her knuckles turned white. "How long will he need to eat this way?"

"Just for a week or so. Then we'll decide what to do after that."

"Dina, would you mind making a fresh pot of coffee?" Cade picked up the nearly empty pot and held it out to her. "I'd appreciate it."

"Of course, of course." Geraldine jumped to her feet and grabbed the pot out of Cade's hand. "It will take a few minutes."

Once she was out of earshot, Cade sent Abby such an intense look she felt pinned to the back of her chair.

"You think it something he's eating that's causing this?"

"I'm not sure," Abby admitted. "But the pattern fits something he's exposed to or eats regularly, but not all the time."

"Who are you going to send with this special broth?" Cade asked.

"Cook. That is, he's a cook, but that's…"

"Also his name," Cade finished her sentence, much to Abby's surprise.

"He works for Charles," Cade continued. "And looks after Jamison's niece."

"Ammie." Abby nodded while she gathered up her tapestry bag and placed it in her lap. "Cook rescued Lillian and then raised her, and now he looks after the household of Charles's sister and their niece."

"Will he hurt Dina's feelings with this recipe of his on how to prepare the broth?"

"Of course not," Abby said, crossing her fingers beneath her bag. She mentally added, *please be kind to Geraldine,* to the talk she'd have with Cook later that morning.

Cade eyed her bag. "Were you thinking of leaving before we had our talk?"

Abby stood up and frowned at him. "We've been talking for an hour, and I do have other patients to see. I'll be back in a few days to look in on Jules. If he has another attack before then, please send for me at once." She took out a neatly printed card and set it on the table next to her chair. "This is my direction. Just send me word and I'll come as soon as I can."

"Not so fast, Abagail." Cade stood as well and crossed his arms over his chest.

That's not a good sign, she thought, barely registering that he'd used her given name.

"Now let's talk about the Linder gang."

Abby's mouth dropped open. She had no idea why the marshal had brought up that particular topic. The gang needed to be stopped, and Cade McKenzie was a US Marshal. What more was there to discuss?

"What about the Linder gang?" she asked cautiously, wondering what he was after.

"I haven't caught them yet."

"All right," Abby said, adding an encouraging smile. "But I'm sure you will."

She didn't appreciate the sudden look of amusement that leapt into his eyes, or the upward twitch of his mouth. She had tried to pay the man a compliment, for goodness sakes, and he looked as if he wanted to burst into laughter.

"I'm sure I will too." Cade grinned for a brief moment before his face settled into the serious expression she was much more accustomed to seeing.

"But until then, you aren't to go out and about at night without an escort, and you aren't to leave the city."

"Really? Would I be breaking the law?" Abby asked, injecting a tinge of acid into her voice. The man had no right to tell her what she could and couldn't do, even if he was a marshal. He had his job and she had hers—which included seeing her patients whenever and wherever they needed her.

"It's just plain common sense, Dr. Metler." Cade's jaw tightened as he continued to pin her with his stare.

"I see. Well, I shall most certainly keep that in mind, Marshal McKenzie." Abby deliberately smiled. "I'm late for my first appointment this morning. Please be sure to give Geraldine my card."

Without another word or backwards glance, she breezed through the parlor and right out the front door before he could stop her. She was settling into the seat of her buggy just as he appeared on the porch. Giving him a polite nod, because after all, she wasn't a rude person, Abby snapped the reins and set Daisy into motion.

* * *

Hours later, Abby closed the medical book and placed it on the small table next to her rocking chair. Maggie's husband, Ian, had made the chair just for her, and she absolutely adored it. It was her favorite place to read, but tonight she simply couldn't concentrate.

After a busy day of seeing patients, and arranging for Cook to deliver a simple broth and plainly cooked chicken for Jules, she had stopped at her cousin's house to pick up a basket with her own dinner tucked away inside, thanks to her cousin's housekeeper. Lillian had been taking a cup of tea in the kitchen, and Abby had happily accepted the invitation to join her. She had definitely been in the mood for a cozy chat.

The doctor had spent the next hour talking about Jules, and Geraldine, and especially one Cade McKenzie. The man had told her—no ordered her—to stay in town and take an escort with her everywhere. She was a physician, for goodness sakes. Her patients couldn't wait while she flitted about and made arrangements for some sort of guard simply to keep Marshal McKenzie happy.

Every time Lillian nodded her agreement, Abby had felt justified in airing more complaints about the man. She'd added another teaspoon of sugar to her tea as she'd methodically listed all his many shortcomings. Hadn't he walked off with barely a "goodbye", leaving poor Paul's dinner scattered all over the sidewalk? And then couldn't even bother to remember her name? Why, he even implied she thought his cousin's cooking was poisoning his brother, when she'd never said any such thing. The marshal would try the patience of a saint, and the only reasonable thing she could do to keep their acquaintance civil was to avoid him as much as possible. In fact, the more she thought about it, she should only deal with Geraldine. There was no need for her to see the insufferable Cade McKenzie at all.

Satisfied with that conclusion, Abby had set her teacup aside to give Lillian a hug before making her way home on foot. She always left Daisy and the carriage in Lillian's stable for Danny or Little Jake to look after. The quick ten-minute walk to her cozy home just down the hill helped clear her head. Her cottage used to be Maggie's dress shop, until the Irish seamstress needed to find a larger space. Ian had first built it for his wife's business, and then completely redone the inside to turn it into a perfect fit for Abby.

She loved coming home every night. The stone fireplace warmed the front two rooms, the larger of which served as her parlor, with a comfy divan and several chairs. Lovely, vibrant paintings of the beautiful bay hung on the walls. As welcoming as the parlor was, Abby spent most of her time in the room on the other side of the tiny foyer. Ian had surprised her with her own, personal library. The walls were lined with shelves, which she'd had no trouble filling to the brim with books. Under the front window was a writing desk, and in the other corner her beloved rocking chair and side table. She was happiest when she was in this room, and felt perfectly content with the thought of living in her little cottage forever.

But tonight she wasn't finding it quite as restful as she usually did. And all because of a bossy US Marshal. Another thing to add to her long list of complaints about Cade McKenzie.

A sharp knock on the front door had Abby jumping out of her rocker. She stood for a moment, breathing rapidly, a hand pressed to her chest. She could feel her heart racing beneath her fingertips.

"Doctor Abby? Are you in there? Doctor Abby?"

Abby's eyes widened and her pulse kicked even higher when she recognized the voice. Miguel. It was Miguel from the ranch. There was no reason for him to be in town, especially at this time of night, unless…

Praying nothing horrible had happened to one of the children, Abby ran to the front door and threw it open. Reaching up to push her spectacles firmly back into place, she stared at the young man with the dark hair and dark eyes, standing in front of her, holding his hat in his hand. He was covered in dust.

"Miguel, what's happened?"

"Doctor Abby, you need to come quick. It's Mister George. He's hurt bad. Some men shot him."

"Shot?" Abby gasped. She grabbed onto the front of Miguel's shirt and pulled him into the foyer. "When?"

"This morning, sometime just before noon."

Abby did a quick mental calculation. She needed to go to the ranch right now. Organizing tasks in her mind, she picked up her medical bag, which she always kept near the front door.

"Ride to Miss Lillian's. You know where she lives, don't you?" She waited half a heartbeat for Miguel's nod. "Tell young Jake to saddle Marron, and put on an extra saddlebag. I'll be right behind you."

She gave him a light push. "Go, Miguel.

Chapter Six

"Gone? What do you mean she's gone?" Cade's good mood from enjoying a comfortable, uninterrupted night's sleep instantly soured. Jules had had his first night in a month without suffering from one of his breathing attacks. The marshal knew he owed the doctor more than just a simple "thank you". And not being able to tell her that put a fierce scowl on his face.

It was midmorning before he'd managed to carve out time to stop by Abagail's office. He was well aware she wasn't happy with his order to stay in town unless she had a guard with her. She'd then run off before he'd had a chance to make his reasons clear, although it should have been plain enough to her. He could have easily chased her down, and usually would have since it was his way to settle any problem at once rather than let it fester. But he'd thought it best for Abagail to calm down first.

Next time he'd tie her to the nearest piece of furniture before he allowed her to walk off when she was angry with him.

Dr. Melton lifted his cane and thumped it on the seat of the visitor's chair in his office. "Why don't you sit, young man. You look like you're about to explode."

Cade impatiently shifted his weight from one foot to the other. "Where is Abagail?"

The older man's thick eyebrows drew together. "Abagail, is it?"

"Where is she?" Cade repeated, ignoring the doctor's question. They could argue the proprieties later. Right now he wanted answers.

"Are you going to sit?" the doctor asked.

Cade touched a hand to his cheek and continued to stare at the man leaning heavily on his cane.

With a deep sigh Dr. Melton reached across his desk and picked up a sheet of paper. "I assume she left sometime last night. She wrote a note."

When Cade held out his hand, the older man shook his head. "If Abby meant for you to read this, she'd have put your name on it."

Completely out of patience, Cade opened his mouth, snapping it shut again when the doctor loudly cleared his throat.

"But, there's nothing in here that says I cannot read it to you." He adjusted his spectacles and looked at the paper in his hand. "Says something happened at the ranch and she needs to get there as soon as possible. Let's see now. There's a list of supplies Miguel will pick up at some time later today. Doesn't know how long she'll be gone. I'm to pay a visit to Jules McKenzie..." The doctor paused and looked at Cade over the upper rim of his spectacles. "I'm assuming that's your brother?" At Cade's short nod, he returned his gaze to the paper. "If I need anything more, I'm to send word to Lillian. And then she wrote, 'if the marshal stops by, tell him I haven't done anything illegal'."

The doctor glanced at Cade. "I gather you understand what that means?"

Cade ignored that question too. But he certainly meant to take it up with Abagail. Once he caught up with her. And he would.

He glanced at the paper on the desk, but it was too far away for him to make out any of the words. "What happened at this ranch that she had to leave in the middle of the night?"

"Marshal, if I knew that I would have said so. I told you what the note says—something happened out at the ranch. Must have been a serious emergency for her to leave so suddenly."

57

"Did she go by herself?" Cade drew in a slow breath against the hard weight forming in the pit of his stomach. Surely the woman hadn't been that reckless?

Dr. Melton pursed his lips and took a full step backwards. "She didn't say. But I suspect you know the answer to that."

"Where is this ranch?" Cade snapped the words out.

He gritted his teeth when the man across from him smiled. "You'd best put that question to Lillian. The ranch belongs to her, and she's the one who should decide if you're welcome there."

The marshal clenched his fists and tamped down the urge to beat the information out of the man. "Lillian is Charles Jamison's wife?"

"That's right." The doctor nodded. "Which is why I'm sending you to *The Crimson Rose,* Charles' gaming establishment, and I imagine you've been in town long enough to know where that is. It's early in the day for Lillian to be there yet, but if an angry man is wanting to talk to his wife, Charles should be told. And I warn you. If you do anything to threaten her, the man won't hesitate to shoot you, even if you are a US Marshal."

"I don't threaten women." Cade turned on his heel and left the office, slamming the door behind him.

***

Twenty minutes later, Cade strode through the wide double doors of *The Crimson Rose*. The gambling hall was one of the more elegant establishments in the city, set in an easily accessible location within the infamous Barbary Coast.

Close to the water, and not far from the town square, the most notorious district in San Francisco held every form of entertainment and vice borrowed from seaports all over the world. Boasting rows of gambling houses and saloons, and dotted with residences presided over by madams in gaudy gowns, as well as the barely hidden entrances to opium dens, the Barbary Coast had it all.

The Crimson Rose catered to the more upscale clientele. It had a spectacular, and ornate, long bar across one entire wall of a large room. Its open floor was filled with tables for games of chance and skill. Upstairs, gambling was conducted in less noisy settings, with a quiet dining area and private rooms to host high stake players, where fortunes were won and lost every night.

Cade took in the main room with a fast glance, his gaze settling on a young, mop-headed boy industriously sweeping the floor. The marshal quietly approached from behind and tapped him on the shoulder. The boy whirled around, his eyes going wide as a thick lock of black hair bounced against his forehead.

"Where can I find Charles Jamison?"

With his brown eyes as big as saucers, the boy immediately lifted a hand and pointed to a door at the back of the room.

"In the kitchen, sir, but I don't think…"

"Thank you, I appreciate it." Cade didn't wait to hear any more, covering the distance with long, rapid strides. With a quick push on the door he kept right on going down a short hallway, not stopping until he crossed into the large light-filled room at the end.

Cade had an impression of several stoves flanked by open shelves holding dozens of pots, pans and bags of staples. But his attention immediately fixed on a pair of huge tables in the center of the room. Two women, two men and a younger male who'd barely left his boyhood behind, sat on high stools clustered around the nearest table. All of them looked over at Cade when he strode through the door.

He figured the platinum-blond beauty sitting close to the Southern gambler was Lillian, his wife. From the minute he'd hit town, he'd heard about Lillian Smith, the most beautiful woman in the city. But for some strange reason none of his contacts had ever mentioned she was also married to Charles Jamison. He could see for himself the stories of her beauty were true. Even at this hour of the morning she'd put most women to shame. However, at the moment he was only interested in one woman, and it wasn't Lillian Smith Jamison.

He walked over to the table and stood at one end, his stare on the blond with the crystal-blue eyes looking back at him.

"Are you Lillian Jamison?"

Cade thought he should have attempted a gentler tone when Charles instantly rose to his feet, putting himself between the marshal and his wife.

"What do you want?" There was no mistaking the threat in the gambler's voice.

Forcing himself to relax, Cade placed both hands flat on top of the table. "I'd appreciate it if I could talk to your wife." That's as far as he got before something cold and hard poked him in the back. He went completely still. Cade was all too familiar with the feel of the barrel of a shotgun.

"Why?" The one word was more a demand than a question.

Now John got to his feet. "Cook, he's the marshal we've been talking about."

Cook? Thinking he should have known, since the only person missing from this gathering was the all-around houseman, Cade briefly closed his eyes. "I'm Cade McKenzie. Jules's older brother."

"Nice boy. I like your cousin, too. She's a kind woman." The shotgun gave him another poke. "Still haven't heard why you want to talk to Lillian."

"Oh for heaven's sake, Cook. Put the gun down. He wants to know about Abby." Lillian's voice floated out from behind her husband's broad back.

"What about Abagail?"

When the poke was repeated, Cade's jaw tightened as he fought to hold onto his temper.

A rustle of skirts followed as both women stood, each giving the men standing in front of them a good shove. John

Davis turned and frowned at the auburn-haired woman who frowned right back at him.

"As long as there's a gun out and pointing in our general direction, you stay behind me, Beth."

"There's a US Marshal between us and that gun," Beth said before raising her voice a notch. "Which Cook should put down. The man is probably here about the shooting. Or Abby." She glanced over at Cade. "Or maybe both?"

The weight in the pit of Cade's stomach got heavier. "What shooting?"

Beth looked over at Lillian. "Uh oh."

Lillian immediately stepped around Charles. When she leaned against his side, her husband slipped an arm around her waist. Lillian smiled up at him before turning her attention back to the tall man with the jagged scar, his deep-blue stare glued to her face.

"I'm Lillian Jamison." She gestured across the table. "And that's Beth Davis, John's wife."

Cade nodded without taking his gaze off Lillian.

"As you heard, the person behind you, who is now going to put that shotgun away, is Cook. And this young man," she pointed to the last occupant of the table who'd sat through the whole exchange still as a statue, with his eyes as big as a closed fist. "This is Miguel. He lives on the ranch."

The marshal looked over at Miguel. "You came to get Abagail?"

The boy bobbed his head up and down. "Doctor Abby. Missus Carrie sent me to fetch her right away." His voice trailed off and his shoulders hunched over as his gaze dropped to the tabletop.

"Stop scaring him." Lillian frowned at Cade. "Sit and have a cup of tea and we'll discuss our plan with you."

He glanced over at Lillian. "I already have a plan. I just need directions to the ranch."

John sat on a stool and pulled Beth onto the one next to him, keeping her hand firmly in his. "We're getting together the supplies Abby wants, and will be sending them along with an armed guard. You're welcome to go with them." He looked over at Charles for confirmation.

Nodding, the gambler leaned over and kissed his wife on her cheek. "Sit down, sweetheart." Once Lillian was settled, Charles turned to Cade.

"I'm sure Luke, my ranch manager, would be glad to have you along. They'll be ready to leave in a couple of hours."

Cade shook his head. "I'm leaving now. I need directions to the ranch."

"Marshal McKenzie," Beth spoke up. "A lone rider in broad daylight isn't going to help matters."

"No, it won't," John agreed.

"Then Abagail wasn't alone?" Cade's relief was short-lived.

"She went alone," John confirmed then held up his hand. "Because she thought Miguel was too tired to make the trip back, and his horse wouldn't be able to keep up with hers."

"That's what she said?" Cade asked the younger man who was still scrunched down on his stool. But he managed to shake his head at Cade's question.

"She didn't tell me anything except to have Marron saddled," Miguel said.

"Then how…?" Cade was interrupted by five voices speaking in unison.

"She left a note."

"Of course she did," he muttered under his breath. The woman apparently thought scratching out a note made everything just dandy and fine.

Lillian looked around the table and nodded at the others. "She told me that Miguel was too tired to ride back with her and I could get the story of what happened from him. And that she was leaving at once on Marron, and she'd send word as soon as George could have visitors." Lillian paused to smile at the question in Cade's eyes. "Marron is her horse, and George is the ranch foreman. His wife, Carrie, takes care

62

of the children and the house. Abby also wrote out a list of supplies for Charles, and left another note for Beth asking her to please take Maggie over to her cottage and pack a few clothes, since she may be gone a week or so, and to ask John to send a guard with the driver for the supplies. Her final note was for Cook, with instructions about your brother."

Cade rolled his eyes and put "writing notes" on his growing, mental list of things to discuss with Miss Abagail Metler.

"Was it the foreman who was shot? I'm assuming that's why she wanted a guard for the wagon driver?" Cade asked.

Now Cook stepped forward, placing a fresh cup of tea in front of Lillian and taking the seat next to her. The man was tall and stick thin, with spindly arms, long legs and a deadly stare. Not quite the picture Cade had in his mind for a cook, housekeeper and nanny. He was also very protective of Lillian. *Like a father*, Cade thought.

"Before you start peppering the boy with questions, let's get the whole thing out," Cook said. "The shooting wasn't an accident. George was still conscious when they found him. He said he was attacked by a group of men when he was out checking on the cattle and came across a partially slaughtered steer. It was shot in the head, and George is very fortunate those men didn't do the same to him. Miguel and two of the older boys found him a few hours later with a hole in his side. They managed to get him home, and Carrie got the bleeding stopped, but needed Abagail to take the bullet out and deal with any infection."

Cook paused and gave the marshal a good once-over look, from head to toe. "That horse of Abagail's came from Rayne's ranch up north. She knows how to breed them. Marron can outrun most other horses, which Abagail has had to do a time or two."

The spider-like Cook opened his hand and shoved the folded sheet of paper he was holding across the table toward Cade. "Here are directions to the ranch."

63

John took one look at Cade's face and pursed his lips when he glanced over at Cook. "You aren't helping."

"Nonsense," Cook said as Cade snatched the piece of paper and went out the door. The former sailor smiled at his retreating back. "Having all the facts will likely make the man ride that much harder. Now, I need to get back to my work before I check on Jules and Miss Geraldine. All of you should stop by their home and introduce yourselves, in case they need something while the marshal is gone."

"Yes, Cook" echoed around the table as the former seaman headed for the door, a smile on his face.

Charles shrugged and looked over at John. "I don't know what Cook was thinking. McKenzie might run his horse into the ground chasing after Abby, and we'll end up having to send a search party out for him.

Charles stood and rolled his shoulders. "We'd better check on the supplies."

Nodding his agreement, John leaned over and gave his wife a quick kiss before following the gambler out the door.

Beth grinned at her friend. "Think the marshal will ride a bit harder?"

"Maybe." Lillian glanced over at her friend, a definite sparkle in her eye. "Abby stopped by last evening and had a cup of tea."

"Tea? She doesn't even like tea," Beth said.

"She was so intent on complaining about the marshal, I don't think she had any idea what she was drinking. Along with her complaints, she also gave a very thorough description of Cade McKenzie. Including how tall he was, the blue of his eyes, his smile and his voice. She spouted off enough details to make me wonder just what was going on with her and the marshal."

"He's a good-looking man," Beth observed. "Could be nothing more than that."

Lillian shook her head. "There's something more than that. I knew it was the marshal the minute he walked in the door. Charles gave a good description of him, but Abby's was perfect, except…"

"Except what?" Beth demanded when her friend paused.

Leaning over, Lillian dropped her voice to a conspiratorial whisper. "She never mentioned his scar."

Beth laughed. "Well, they do say love is blind."

Chapter Seven

Abby stood up, first stretching her back and then giving her shoulders a hard rub with her fingertips. It felt as if she'd bent over the bed George was sleeping in for hours. Which, of course, was true.

It had taken what was left of the night before, and almost until noon that day, to make the trip to the ranch. She'd pushed Marron through the night as much as she'd dared, and even more when the sun came over the horizon, so they'd both arrived dusty, dirty and exhausted. Her feet were barely on the ground when Carrie had flown across the wide front porch. Abby had managed to grab her bag before the frantic woman had dragged her into the house and back to the bedroom where her husband lay. He'd looked as white as the sheet pulled up over his chest, which rose and fell with his rapid, short gasps of air.

Not wasting any time, Abby had set everyone into motion, tearing bandages, boiling water and fetching clean bed sheets. Two hours later the bullet was removed, the wound properly sealed and bandaged, and the patient resting as peacefully as he could be considering he had a bullet hole in his side. The normally unflappable Carrie, with her solid build and streaks of gray in her hair, had clutched the back of a chair just to remain on her feet.

Abby had firmly insisted the matron get some rest, declaring there was nothing more to do but wait and see if any infection set in. Carrie had been reluctant, but finally gave in after Abby had promised to rouse her the minute her husband woke up. Which had led to another round of promises that the doctor was sure George would indeed open his eyes again.

For the next several hours Abby had sat by the bedside, listening to her patient's breathing and periodically checking his wound. Every few minutes one or more of the children had peeked into the room. A couple had bravely asked how he was doing, while the smaller ones had simply stared at the figure in the bed.

As the evening set in, Abby was rapidly approaching a full day and night without sleep. Wobbling on her feet, she sat back in the chair she'd pulled up alongside the bed before she fell into a heap on the floor. Which didn't sound like such a bad thing. She was so tired it would be heaven to simply curl up on the floor and close her eyes.

"How is he?" Carrie whispered, tiptoeing into the room in her stocking feet.

"He's doing very well," Abby said. "You should get more rest."

"Got as much as I need."

Abby turned slightly and adjusted her spectacles. Carrie did look much better after her three-hour nap. Her shoulders no longer drooped halfway to the ground, and her brown eyes had lost most of their redness. Nodding her approval, Abby looked back to her patient.

"So far, he's only a little warm, nothing to worry about. I've kept cold cloths on his forehead."

"I can do that. You go on and lie down now. I'll sit with him." When Abby didn't immediately agree, Carrie crossed her arms over her ample bosom and peered at the doctor. "I fixed up a room right next door for you. The small ones can sleep with the older ones in the loft for a while. Be a nice treat for them. If I holler, you'll be able to hear me."

Knowing she couldn't go on much longer without rest, Abby finally nodded. With a supreme effort, she managed to get to her feet.

"Be sure to, um, holler if there's any change at all."

Carrie put an arm around Abby's waist and walked with her to the bedroom next door. It had a tall dresser in one corner, a wardrobe in another, and a wide bed frame with a mattress, which was topped by several neatly folded quilts, and jutted out from the far wall into the center of the room.

"You're dead on your feet, honey. You just lie down there and close your eyes. We'll be all right now, thanks to you."

Abby did exactly as she was told, crawling onto the feather tick without even removing her riding boots. Before the grateful matron could blink, the doctor was sound asleep.

Making a clucking noise, Carrie drew a quilt over the woman she considered a true godsend, before quietly exiting the room.

***

Cade moved cautiously through the brush, slowly making his way up a small hill. He was sure he'd spotted a campfire just up ahead, a short distance from the road leading to the ranch he'd been scouting for the last hour.

He stopped for a moment, getting a feel for the land and the night itself. He judged it wasn't long past midnight, and as far as he could tell the ranch was as quiet as a church on a Monday morning. There was no sign of anyone stirring except for the glow of a campfire he'd spotted from the road, and the one just like it on the far side of the corral. It took another two minutes of moving through the dark before he spotted the small fire again, flickering against the rocks set into the hillside. But he didn't see anyone.

Cade worked his way closer to the fire, skirting just beyond its ring of light. A pair of small, pinto ponies stamped their hooves when he passed them. They didn't make any other protest, but went back to chomping on the stray tufts of grass dotting the area. He'd only gotten to the quarter point when he stopped and listened. A faint sound came from the rocks to his left. Cade rolled his eyes when he recognized the noise.

He could hear the snoring from a good twenty feet away.

As soon as he rounded one of the boulders he spotted two figures, both leaning against the rock with rifles drooping over the sides of their arms. He judged they were younger than the other two he'd located, and were supposed to be keeping an eye out for any intruders. Cade's jaw clenched at the thought that these children were the only protection the ranch, and Abagail, had.

Sighing, he quietly approached until he stood directly behind them. In one smooth motion Cade pulled the rifles up and out of the way. Both boys came awake with small yelps, and a purely comical scramble to get to their feet.

"Give me back my gun," the smallest one shouted, his chin sticking out and his eyes glittering with tears.

"Calm down, boys." Cade leaned both rifles against the rock behind him then faced the two young sentries, looking the diminutive pair over as he crossed his arms over his chest.

"I'm US Marshal Cade McKenzie, on my way to that ranch just up the road. What are you two doing out here?"

"If you're a marshal, where's your badge?" the younger and shorter of the two asked. His eyes narrowed on Cade's chest. "I don't see a badge."

Doing his best not to grin at the boy, who barely came up to the middle of his chest, Cade dug into his vest pocket and pulled out his badge. While the two kids gaped at the gold star, Cade took a quick glance at the road. The moon gave off enough light to see it was empty, with nothing stirring except a light wind.

"We're not doing anything wrong, Marshal, sir." The smaller one seemed to be the leader of the two. "We aren't running away or anything. We're watching, is all."

"What's your name, son?" Cade asked.

The boys looked at each other and then down at the ground. Apparently they thought they were in a heap of trouble. And they should be. But Cade was having a hard time keeping the frown on his face. They looked to be about Jules's age, and damn pathetic with their heads hanging halfway to their knees.

69

"I'm Robbie and he's Billy."

"We're guarding the ranch on account of Mister George be'in shot," Billy blurted out.

"Well, you picked a good place," Cade said. He turned and lifted the rifles, balancing both against one shoulder. "But we need to get you back to the ranch now."

"We gotta watch in case those men come back," Robbie insisted. "We gotta protect Missus Carrie and Doctor Abby until help comes. Doctor Abby said Mister Charles is sure to send help."

Cade stopped and looked at their upturned faces. "Doctor Abby is at the ranch? Is she all right?"

"She ain't hurt if that's what yur askin'," Billy said.

Nodding, Cade touched a hand to his cheek and stared off into the distance, absorbing the wave of relief rolling through him. Abagail made it to the ranch. All he had to do was be sure she got back to town in one piece, where he could keep an eye on her. If he didn't kill her first for putting him through this mad race across the hills.

"Let's go, boys. Mister Charles sent me, so that makes me your help." It was true enough since Charles approved of him coming along. Cade just hadn't waited for the rest of the men.

Thirty minutes later, the threesome pulled up in front of the ranch house. Billy slid off his horse first, waving at the woman standing on the porch, a shotgun in her hand. Cade wondered if he had to take another weapon away from one of the ranch residents before they hurt themselves, or anyone else. Namely him.

"Missus Carrie. We found a marshal," Robbie called out, leaping down from his mount. "His name is Cade Kinzie, and he's here to help."

"Hush up, Robbie, before you wake the whole place with your yellin'."

The woman moved out of the shadows and into the moonlight. Cade figured by the way she held that shotgun, she knew how to use it. He touched one finger to the brim of his hat.

"Ma'am. I'm Marshal McKenzie. Charles Jamison sent me."

Carrie lowered the shotgun until the barrel touched the ground. "I've heard of you. Doctor Abby mentioned you. She said your manners needed some work."

Knowing better than to argue with a woman holding a gun, Cade inclined his head toward his two young companions. "Found these boys up in the hills. They were watching the road leading into the ranch. Did you send them up there?"

"I most certainly did not," Carrie said.

She set the gun aside and marched down the porch steps. Cade coughed to cover his laugh when Robbie muttered an "uh oh," behind him. The woman kept on coming, and didn't stop until she was directly in front of Cade.

"I'll take those rifles," she said, holding out her hand.

Cade lifted the guns off his shoulder and handed them to her.

"Now you two boys take the horses, including the marshal's, and put them away before you get yourselves back to bed. And don't let me catch you roaming about the ranch at night again. Do you hear me?"

"Yes ma'am." Both boys bobbed their heads before grabbing a handful of lead reins and pulling the horses toward the barn.

Once they were out of earshot, Cade cleared his throat. "There's another pair of boys alongside a gulch about a half mile that way," Cade pointed in the opposite direction from the way he'd come into the ranch. "I circled the hills around the house. There isn't anyone coming tonight, so the boys should be safe until daylight."

Sighing heavily, Carrie shook her head. "I'll have to take your word on that. I can't go out to fetch them and leave my husband and the children alone here. Our two ranch hands are out guarding the cattle."

Cade thought he needed to have a talk with those two hands about obeying foolish orders. Protecting the women and children was more important than watching over cattle. But right now, he had something else to deal with.

"You said Doctor Abby is here?"

Carrie squinted up at him in the dark. "Is she the reason you rode all this way?"

Too tired to bother with any pretense, Cade simply nodded. "Is she inside?"

"She's sleepin'. You can too, marshal. The boys have some nice places fixed up in the barn."

"Thank you, ma'am. I'll just check on Abagail first."

"Suit yourself." Carrie turned and headed for the house with Cade following her. Once inside the large main room, he took off his hat and held it to his side, taking a curious look around while Carrie put the rifles up on the pegs next to the front door.

At least a dozen chairs were scattered around, most clustered near the fireplace. A large table with two long wooden benches stood next to a wide archway leading into another room that Cade suspected was the kitchen. Carrie came up beside him and briefly touched his arm.

"I'm goin' to sit with my husband. Doctor Abby's in that room there, but mind you leave that door open while you're doin' your checkin'. And don't you wake her up, neither. She's tuckered out after ridin' all night, then takin' a bullet out of George."

"No, ma'am. I won't wake her."

While Carrie moved off, Cade strode over to the door she'd pointed to and slowly eased it open. The single skinny window in the bedroom let in just enough light he could see the mound of covers on the bed, and a pair of boots sticking out from beneath them. Moving quietly, he walked over and stared down at Abby's face. In the sprinkle of moonlight, with her long lashes lying against her cheek, she looked like an angel.

Since looking and acting were two different things, Cade shook his head at the thought before glancing around until he spied a rocking chair. He retrieved it from the corner and carried it over to the bed. Taking off his rain slicker, he draped it over the bed post before carefully lowering his weight onto the chair. Satisfied it would hold, he lifted his boots to the top of the mattress and settled them next to Abby's before closing his eyes.

Chapter Eight

Abby opened her eyes and frowned at the rough-hewn beams crisscrossing the ceiling of her room. Still groggy and disoriented, she peeked over the edge of the quilt and looked around the unfamiliar surroundings. It took a full minute to remember she was at the ranch and in one of the bedrooms in the main house. In that same minute, she remembered her patient and flung away the heavy coverlet. Still half-asleep, she started to reach for her robe, then looked at her feet when they made a solid "clunk" as they hit the floor. Her boots were still on. Running a hand over her lopsided braid, she decided to deal with putting herself properly together after she'd checked on George.

Since her bedroom door was wide open, she simply walked out and turned left into the next room. Carrie looked up and smiled from her place near the bed. Abby's answering smile grew wider when she saw George was awake. He even gave her a weak nod.

Carrie rose and moved aside as Abby hurried over.

"How is he?" she asked as she picked up George's wrist and began counting the beats, along with the seconds on the pocket watch she'd left on the bedside table the night before.

"He's doing fine," Carrie said, placing a gentle hand on Abby's shoulder. "Thanks to you."

The doctor finished counting off the full minute before gently releasing the ranch foreman's arm and turning to look at his wife. "Mostly to you, Carrie. You're the one who stopped the bleeding and kept him alive."

"He's not deaf or dead. I can hear you both." George's voice came out in a low croak.

Abby leaned over the bed and placed the back of her hand on his forehead. Nodding with satisfaction, she pushed the covers aside and lifted the bandage over the wound enough to check its color and take a discreet sniff for any rancid odor.

"You don't feel too hot. We still need to give it another day, but so far, no infection has set in." She smiled and patted his arm. "You're a lucky man, George Cowan."

He managed a weak smile as Abby stepped aside so his wife could sit next to him again.

Once Carrie settled herself in her chair, she wrinkled her nose at Abby's rumpled skirt. "I imagine you'll be wanting a bath. I had the tub set up in Lillian's guesthouse where your spare clothes are."

Abby thought a bath, even a cold one, sounded like heaven.

"Thank you, but you didn't have to go to all that trouble. I could have put up sheets for privacy and used the one on the back porch."

"I didn't set it up," Carrie said, grinning. "But before you get to that bath, you need to take care of your other problem."

"What other problem?" Abby's forehead wrinkled with confusion. As far as she knew, her only problem was lying in the bed recovering nicely.

Carrie tilted her head toward the bedroom door. "The one that followed you here from town. He's at the table, having coffee."

"He?" Abby's mind drew a blank for a moment before her eyes became moon-sized behind her spectacles. "He didn't."

"Oh yes, he did." Carrie nodded.

"Who're you two talkin' about?" George asked.

"Never you mind. I'll tell you later," his wife said before frowning at Abby. "You go on out there and settle whatever the problem is between you."

Not trusting herself to say another word, Abby turned and walked the few steps to the doorway. Sure enough, Cade McKenzie was sitting at the long table. He nodded and raised a tin mug in her direction.

Abby reached back and closed the bedroom door behind her. She didn't want to bother her patient when she told the marshal to go home. He had no business following her around. She forced herself to keep to a sedate walk. Once she was standing in front of him, she put her hands on her hips and carefully looked him over.

He clearly was tired, with dark circles etched beneath his eyes. But his color was good, he wasn't slumping across the table, and she could see for herself that all his limbs were still attached. He was so new to the area, she really was relieved he'd made the trip to the ranch in one piece. Since she expected the supply wagon from Charles and Lillian today, Cade McKenzie could make the trip back when they returned to town. And she intended to tell him precisely that. She'd make her own way home once George was out of danger and safely on the mend.

Having worked everything out in her mind, she pasted a smile on her face and belatedly returned his nod.

"I'm surprised to see you, Marshal McKenzie. Are you out here to look into the shooting?"

Cade snorted and set his coffee mug down. "I will be, but that's not the reason I'm here, Dr. Metler."

"Well, whatever your business is, I hope you'll be able to conclude it in time to return with the supply wagon. It should be here close to sundown, I think." Abby kept her tone politely formal and her smile in place.

Sighing, Cade stood up. "If we're going to have a fight, I prefer to have it in private."

"We are not…" Abby let out a yelp when the man picked her up. Too startled to think what she was doing, Abby flung her arms around his neck to keep from tumbling to the ground.

"What are you doing, Cade McKenzie?" She kicked her feet but he had a firm grip around her legs. "Where are we going? You put me down right now."

Cade tipped his chin to his chest and looked at her. "In a minute."

Abby clamped her mouth shut and fumed. He strode through the house, entering the kitchen where several of the children were peeling vegetables. They all turned big eyes and open mouths toward Cade, and the woman he was carrying.

"Children," Abby said nodding, doing her best to look as if nothing unusual was going on.

"I need to have a private talk with Doctor Abby that might get loud. You kids go out on the front porch for a while."

Without a word, paring knives were abandoned and the kitchen was empty within seconds.

"You certainly do enjoy giving orders. And I don't get loud," Abby muttered, then quickly ducked her head closer to Cade's shoulder as he maneuvered them both through the narrow doorway leading from the kitchen to the wide back porch.

Kicking the door shut behind him, Cade set Abby on her feet. He stepped back and crossed his arms over his chest. "Care to explain why you rode like a crazy woman across the country by yourself?"

Abby narrowed her blue eyes and crossed her own arms. "Obviously my patient had an emergency. Which makes me a doctor, not a crazy woman."

Cade's jaw went tight. Never a good sign. But Abby wasn't in the mood to placate the man.

"If you didn't come to investigate the shooting, would you kindly tell me why you're here? And you're the crazy person to go riding alone across country you don't know at all. You're lucky you still aren't wandering about the hills and then we would have had to have sent a search party after you."

"That, Abagail, would never happen," Cade said. "And I'm here because I was chasing after you, and you well know it."

Abby did know it, but was surprised at the spurt of warmth traveling through her to hear him say it. Not that she'd ever admit such a thing to Cade McKenzie. The man had a high enough opinion of himself.

She lifted her shoulders in an exaggerated shrug. "All right, you found me. As you can see, I'm perfectly fine."

Cade blew out a breath and looked off into the distance before backing up two steps and leaning against the porch rail. "I guess it's time for us to have that reasonable talk again."

"Again?" Abby raised an eyebrow.

"The one I tried to have with you back at my house before you walked off in a huff," Cade said.

"I do not walk off in huffs. And a conversation, Marshal McKenzie, involves two people talking with each other," Abby said with a lift of her chin.

"What did you think we were doing, Abagail? I'm pretty sure there were two of us there."

"You giving out orders and expecting me to follow them is not a conversation."

Cade ran a hand through his hair. "I wasn't giving orders."

Abby impatiently tapped her foot. "Oh? What would you call telling me to stay inside unless I have an escort, and to not leave town?"

"Common sense," Cade said.

"As I've explained to you before, Marshal, I have patients."

"Let Dr. Melton take care of them, until I can get this situation resolved."

She rolled her eyes. The man was as stubborn as a mule. "You saw Dr. Melton. He can barely get around. He can't even see his own patients outside of the office, much less mine."

"Then tell your patients to come to the office."

"So Carrie Cowan should have thrown George into a wagon to make the trip into town, with a bullet in his side?"

"A bullet most likely put there by Ben Linder, or one of his gang."

Now Abby snorted. "You can't know that."

"I *can* know that," Cade countered. "George was awake when I looked in on him early this morning. He heard them talking when they thought he was unconscious. They called the leader 'Ben' and another one 'Hal'. It's them all right. And not a mile or two from where you came riding across the hills. Alone."

Abby uncrossed her arms and stared at him. "Then you'd better catch them soon." She turned and started for the backdoor. "I won't argue about this any longer. I need a bath and some clean clothes before I start examining the children."

"This conversation isn't over, Abagail," he warned, pushing away from the porch rail.

"Fine," Abby said. "But right now, I'm going to fetch my bathwater."

Cade strode across the porch and snatched the bucket off its peg before Abby could reach for it.

"I know where the tub's set up. I'll get your water. You go have coffee and a bite to eat. I'll let you know when your bath is ready."

Suddenly realizing she was indeed hungry, Abby still didn't like him ordering her around. "I can get one of the older children to help me. You don't need to tell me what to do as if I'm just out of pinafores."

Cade faced her and touched one hand to his cheek. "Then don't stand there and pout."

Abby immediately pulled in her bottom lip. She was not pouting. Well, not much.

"And I'm not ordering you around. I'm helping you with the bath water because that little guesthouse is a ways to lug a heavy bucket, and whether you like it or not, Dr. Metler, I'm not only bigger than you, but stronger. Or didn't you learn that in your medical books?"

"I certainly don't need any lectures on medicine, Marshal," Abby retorted.

"No, you don't. But what you *do* need is to learn common sense. Either that, or a keeper to make sure you stay where you're put... or a husband foolish enough to take on the job." Cade threw out that last comment before descending the porch steps, heading in the direction of the well on the far side of the barn.

Abby stood watching him, her mouth open and her hands on her hips. A keeper or a husband? She glared at his back as he walked away with those easily recognizable, long strides of his. It was a thoroughly outrageous thing to say to her.

The man really had no manners at all.

Chapter Nine

Noon was fast approaching when Abby finished checking over the last of the dozen children living on the ranch. Thankfully, she'd found nothing to worry over except a few scrapes and bruises. And as usual, the girls were sweet and chatty and the boys squirmed to get away, accompanied by mischievous grins. Robbie raced outside the minute she'd pronounced him healthy as ever. She'd smiled thinking how he reminded her of a slightly younger Jules McKenzie. So much so, that maybe she should find a way to get the two boys together.

She pondered that possibility while re-packing her medical bag. It wasn't two minutes later that Robbie came running back inside, slamming the door behind him.

Carrie looked up from the dishes she was washing and frowned at the young boy. "Robbie, you mind how you come into this house."

"There's some wagons and men coming down the hill," Robbie announced.

"What did that boy say?" George yelled through the open door to his bedroom. A moment later came the sounds of rustling blankets, along with a few grunts and groans.

"Now you stay right where you are," Carrie answered, grabbing a drying rag as she scurried across the room.

Abby hurried over to an excited Robbie and clamped a hand over his mouth. "It's only the supplies. Don't get Mister George all concerned."

Robbie cast a glance over to the bedroom where the hollering was coming from, then back to Abby before nodding.

Abby dropped her hand to his thin shoulder and gave it a gentle squeeze. "Go wait for them on the front porch. I'll be out in a minute."

As he raced away again, Abby crossed over to the doorway. "Calm down, George. I doubt if a gang of thieves would be wandering about in broad daylight with wagons in tow. I'm sure it's the supplies I asked for."

"What supplies? We aren't due to get any until the end of the month," George said, scooting himself higher up on the pillows.

"Just a few things for our medical chest, and new books for the children," Abby assured him.

"We don't need any of that. Can't store the books you and Beth have already sent out here. You should have skipped that and brought a couple of men to protect you when you made the trip here," George groused. "I know you won't be goin' back with the wagons. You never do."

"Stop complainin'," Carrie ordered. "Doctor Abby saved your life. You should be thankin' her, not fussin' at her."

George glared at his wife. "Fussin' is a female thing, Carrie. I'm just sayin' she should be more careful and worry about herself, and not a wagon of damn supplies we don't need until the end of the month. It's no wonder Charles is gettin' gray hair over our Doctor Abby. So am I. So are you, for that matter."

When Carrie gasped and slammed her chubby fists onto her hips, Abby rolled her eyes.

"Glad to see you're much better, George." She smiled at Carrie. "Insulting your wife is a good sign."

"I didn't insult my wife," George insisted.

"You said I was gettin' old."

"I said nothin' like that."

Abby backed quietly away. She was still thinking about what George had said when she stepped out onto the front porch where Robbie was hanging over the rail. The boy was stretched out so far, he was in danger of toppling over the side. Abby joined him and grabbed onto the back of his shirt. Her gaze searched through the men gathered in the yard, but she didn't see Cade anywhere.

Mitch, one of the two hands George hired to help with the heavier work around the ranch, strolled over and leaned against the boards at her feet. He was a good twenty years older than Abby, with a face marked with deep wrinkles, and permanently darkened by the sun.

"Glad you made it here, Doctor Abby." He cast a brief smile in her direction but his gaze never left the approaching wagons. "I thought you'd have a couple of those men riding along when Missus Carrie sent for you. You shouldn't make that trip alone. Worries everyone here, and everyone back in town, too, I suspect."

"I've made the trip by myself before, Mitch," Abby reminded him.

"Didn't like it much then either. Especially don't like it when there's shooting going on."

Giving up, she changed the subject. "You're sure those are the supply wagons and men sent by Charles?"

"If they weren't, we'd 'uv heard from your marshal friend by now," Mitch said.

Startled, Abby stared at the older ranch hand. "Cade isn't here?"

Mitch shrugged. "In a manner of speaking. He's riding the hills around the ranch."

"Looking for whoever shot George? And he's by himself?" Abby's voice rose until she ended on a squeak.

Mitch stared at her. "That's what marshal's do. The go looking for bad men. I suspect this particular marshal has done it before by himself."

Having her own words echoed back to her didn't make Abby feel any better. Something else to discuss with Cade McKenzie. If he ever came out of the hills, that is.

Now both annoyed and frightened, Abby stomped down the porch steps and out into the yard. With her foot tapping against its packed-down surface, she waited for the approaching wagons to pull up in front of the barn.

One of the dust-covered riders dismounted and shouldered his rifle. When he turned to smile at her, Abby laughed and raised her hand in a friendly wave. She'd recognize that grin no matter how much it was disguised by dirt and grime. Lucas Donovan had broken hearts all over the city, and probably during the entire trip from his native Indiana to the Pacific coast.

He'd come to San Francisco to follow his younger brother Ian's example and make a life in a new land. Maggie's brother-in-law was not only a real charmer, he was also the new ranch manager Charles had hired to find the perfect piece of land, and then oversee building a home for Lillian.

Abby was well aware their friends and family thought she and Luke were a perfect match. It was too bad, really, that she and Luke didn't see it that way as well. But it had sparked a few candid conversations between Abby and Luke on how to manage the lot of them, with Luke admitting his sister-in-law, Maggie, was the most persistent matchmaker.

Their common goal to avoid matrimony, at least to each other, had led to a special friendship she enjoyed very much. And right now she was happy to see a friendly face. One she could talk to about anything. In that respect, Luke was like Lillian, Beth, Abby and Rayne. The thought of Luke's reaction, if he knew he was just "another one of her close lady friends", had Abby laughing out loud. She could imagine the look of horror on his face if he ever discovered that comparison.

Luke took a slow walk across the yard and Abby met him halfway. He reached out and gave her a one-armed bear hug, and a quick kiss on the cheek.

"Glad to have caught up with our little rabbit." He grinned at her.

"Oh, not you, too," Abby complained. "I've heard enough of that from Cade to last a lifetime."

Luke stepped back and placed a firm hand on her shoulder. "Cade?"

"Cade McKenzie. Didn't Charles tell you he was coming as well?" Abby asked.

"Are you talking about the marshal? Charles told me I could expect to find a US Marshal here."

Abby nodded. "That would be the currently missing and completely without manners, Cade McKenzie."

"Whoa." Luke held his hand up. "Missing? Without manners? What are you talking about?"

Abby crossed her arms again and proceeded to outline every transgression by Cade, starting with his command not to leave town, all the way through him riding about the hills by himself looking for a gang of killers.

When she'd finished, she reached over and grabbed the sleeve of Luke's shirt. "You should take the men and go find him." Thinking it was a brilliant idea, she tried to tug him back toward the wagons and horses, frowning when Luke dug his heels in and didn't budge.

He shook his head. "I'm not getting on that horse again until I've had some hot coffee and seen the men get something to eat besides jerky and hardtack. But first, tell me how George is doing?"

"He's just fine," Carrie said from behind Abby. "But I'm wantin' to know why the preacher's steppin' off that wagon?"

Abby peered around Luke, squinting through her glass lenses. "That *is* Reverend Hammel."

She turned a questioning look on Luke, who gave both women an easy smile.

"One wagon has the supplies Abby asked for, and the second one has the usual ones Lillian sends every month. They'd be coming out in a week anyway, so we thought to save us a trip. Since the preacher always makes his visit with the monthly supplies, he came along, too."

Abby and Carrie exchanged a glance.

"Well, that was smooth talkin', Luke. And very kind of Lillian to think of it, especially if things had gone different.

But there's no need for any comfortin' or buryin'." Carrie looked past Luke toward the wagons. "Abby and I should look over what you brought. Why don't you go in and see my ornery husband? Let him know you aren't the cattle rustlers who shot him."

Nodding her agreement, Abby gave a shooing motion with her hands. "If you forgot anything, we'll let you know."

Luke loudly groaned as he started for the ranch house, then turned around to walk backwards and grin at her. "You do that, Doctor Abby. And I'll be sure to let *you* know when you can expect to get it."

He gave a short salute when both women laughed before heading up the porch and into the house. His spurs rang as he crossed the hardwood floors, calling out "Where are you at, George? Hiding from the women somewhere?"

"Something I've never seen you do," George growled from his bed.

Chuckling, Luke removed his hat as he stepped inside the snug bedroom. "Taken to lying around in the middle of the day?"

"Only because my wife and Doctor Abby would finish what that bushwhacker started if I didn't."

George held out his hand, which Luke took in a firm grasp.

"Glad he wasn't a better shot," Luke said, smiling at the foreman.

"Hazard of the job. Best you know that now, son," George said before pointing to the chair next to the bed. "Have a seat. Tell me how the trip went."

Luke settled into the chair, placing his hat next to George on the bed. "Not much to tell. Until we got to the yard and I got an earful about the marshal, who I gather is out hunting for the man who shot you."

"He might find the coward, but mostly he was chasin' after Doctor Abby. Didn't like the notion of her comin' by herself. Can't say I much cared for it either."

"Amen to that," Luke agreed. But given Abby's tirade about the marshal, it was interesting to hear.

"I know what the women are hopin', but I don't get the feelin' you and Abby are headin' for gettin' hitched." George shrugged when Luke raised an eyebrow at him.

"Can't say that will make Charles happy," George continued. "He and Lillian are both worried about Abby's safety when she goes out to see her patients. He'd like it fine if a husband would take on that burden. But if you *are* thinkin' along those lines, you might need to hurry up your courtin'."

Luke was about to protest, then thought better of it. He didn't want to disappoint his employer, or his employer's wife, but not enough to get married. However, Abby was like one of the many sisters he left behind on the family farm in Indiana, so he wanted to know all about the man who she might have her eye on.

"Why is that?" he asked, careful to keep his tone casual.

"Got the feelin' Marshal McKenzie comin' after Abby wasn't just part of his job. When he got here, she was sound asleep. He spent the night in a chair by her bedside. In the mornin' he carried her right out of this house to have a private talk with her, which I could hear plain enough since they were on the back porch. And even when she got him riled up, he still toted all that bathwater for her, instead of gettin' the older boys to help. And he set that tub up out in the guest house, too. Heard him tell Carrie he didn't want Abby takin' no bath on a back porch where she might be seen."

"Is that right?" Luke silently sifted through what Abby had told him about the marshal.

George just put her complaints into a whole new light. Luke rubbed the stubble on his chin. He might not need or want a wife, but Abby needed a husband to keep an eye on her. And two things struck him as being real clear. The marshal seemed to want the job, and a preacher could do other things besides give a sermon or say a few words to bury a man.

He leaned back in his chair and grinned at George. "Have I ever told you about my sister, Angie? She couldn't stand my best friend all the years we were growing up. She'd complain about Sam all the time. To listen to her, you'd think she couldn't stand the sight of him. But whenever he'd come around she'd always be there, pestering him about one thing or another. Then one day he came to the door with a big bunch of wildflowers in his hands. Asked her to marry him."

"That sounded like a fool thing to do. She dump those flowers over his head?" George asked.

Luke's grin grew wider. "Nope. She said 'yes'."

Chapter Ten

Luke descended the porch steps, still thinking over the story about his sister and his best friend. Maybe it was just that way with some folks. Too stubborn or near-sighted to see what was right in front of them.

He paused on the last step, considering what he could do to test the marshal's interest in Abby.

The yard was busy. The horse teams were being unhitched by two of the hands, the extra guards he had brought with him were seeing to their mounts or helping unload the wagons, and children ran everywhere while the preacher tried to corral a few of them.

Carrie stood alongside the first wagon with her hands on her hips, giving directions on what to put where. Abby had climbed into the second wagon and was poking through its contents. Luke could imagine her checking off a list she had in her head. His attention shifted when young Robbie suddenly broke free of the preacher and raced across the yard.

He followed the boy's path, spotting the lone rider cantering up the last of the road leading into the ranch. Thanks to Robbie yelling a greeting at the top of his lungs, Luke had no problem identifying the marshal. The very man who was interested in Abby, if George Cowan was to be believed.

Luke studied Cade McKenzie as he drew closer, nodding in satisfaction when the man's gaze did a sweep of the yard, stopping on Abby. While the marshal dismounted and leaned over to listen to whatever it was Robbie was saying, Luke grinned. He wasn't going to pass up an opportunity to find out how the marshal felt about the doctor.

With his gaze fixed on an unsuspecting Abby, Luke strolled across the yard, not stopping until he reached the rear end of the wagon. Hoping he wasn't taking too much of a risk by keeping his back to McKenzie, Luke leaned over the wagon bed.

"Abby? You need to look in on George."

She immediately turned and frowned. "Is something wrong?"

Luke shrugged and held out his hand. "He wants to talk to you. Come on. I'll help you down."

She lifted her skirt and stepped over several bundles of supplies while Luke kept up a chatter, so her attention would stay on him. When she was standing directly over him, giving him a strange look as if she was deciding if he'd spent too much time in the sun, Luke reached up and put his hands around her waist. He easily lifted her off the wagon, deliberately turning so the marshal got a nice side view of the two of them.

Once Abby's feet were on the ground, he kept his hands right where they were, looking down into her upturned face, and adding a smile for good measure. He tried to keep his shoulders and arms from tensing-up when he caught the distinct sound of heavy boot-steps coming their way.

"Luke, my balance is fine. You can let go of me now."

"You heard her."

Luke would have to be stone-deaf not to recognize the menace behind those three little words. With his question about the marshal's interest in Abby answered, and not willing to get his nose smashed in, Luke dropped his hands and faced Cade McKenzie. Since the man's stare was pure, blue ice, Luke thought better of offering a handshake. He liked all his fingers just the way they were, thank you.

"I'm Luke Donovan. Charles sent me with the wagons."

There was a long hesitation before Cade said, "Marshal McKenzie."

The undertones must not have been lost on Abby either, because she stepped away from Luke and closer to the marshal.

"Is something wrong? Did you find the men who shot George?"

Cade switched his gaze to Abby. "No."

When he didn't say anything more, she pursed her lips and narrowed her eyes. "No? Is that all you have to say?"

"No, I didn't find them."

Abby put her hands on her hips, and to Luke's surprise, came damn close to scowling at the marshal. Not something he'd ever seen her do, until now.

"Why did you go out there by yourself?" she demanded.

Cade's brow furrowed. "It's what I do, Abagail. I hunt men who broke the law. And that's a strange thing for *you* to complain about."

She rolled her eyes upward and was silent for a long moment.

Luke thought she was probably counting, trying to hold on to her patience. Having seen and heard all he needed to, he slowly backed away, until he realized he could be screaming like a wildcat and the other two wouldn't have noticed.

Not realizing her friend had deserted her, Abby finished counting to ten and looked back at Cade. "And do you intend to go out *by yourself* again?" She deliberately emphasized "by yourself", just to be sure her point sunk in. Not even Cade McKenzie was that dense.

"Right now I intend to look after my horse." Cade nodded and touched the brim of his hat before he turned around and walked away.

When he led his horse straight into the barn, Abby's mouth dropped open. Apparently the man thought it was fine to give a lecture on *her* behavior at every turn, but didn't think he had to listen to what she had to say regarding the way he went about his business.

Unwilling to leave it at that, Abby huffed out a breath and followed him.

Two of the children came running out just as she reached the door. As they fled past her, Abby shook her head. Now

91

he was scaring the children half to death with that surly glare of his. More determined than ever, she stepped into the shadowed interior, pausing a moment while her eyes adjusted to the dimmer light. It only took that much time for her to locate Cade. He was standing outside the last stall, unsaddling his horse.

As she approached, he slipped the bridle over the animal's head. His horse walked into the stall as Cade hung the bridle on a post nail before turning to look at her.

"What is it now, Abagail?"

"I want to know why you went looking for those men by yourself." She crossed her arms and glared at him. "And don't tell me that's what you do. I know that. But you didn't have to go out alone. Any of the hands would have been happy to accompany you."

Cade snorted. "Accompany me? I wasn't going to a dance, Abagail."

When she continued to glare at him, he ran a hand through his hair and drew in a deep breath. "I wasn't searching for the Linder gang. I was making sure they didn't come around here. There's a difference between hunting and guarding."

Abby thought that over for a few moments. "Why couldn't you do the guarding with someone else along?"

"We're shorthanded. The rest of the men were posted around the ranch."

"Oh. I see." Abby felt heat creep into her cheeks. She really did see why he had gone by himself. But she still didn't like it.

When she said so out loud, Cade's blue eyes grew a shade darker.

"And I didn't like seeing Donovan's hands on you."

"He was just helping me down from the wagon," Abby protested.

Now it was Cade who rolled his eyes. Feeling they were getting nowhere, she tried a different approach. "Maybe we could compromise? You won't go out alone again, and I won't accept Luke's help to climb out of any more wagons."

For the second time Abby's mouth dropped open when Cade strode away. But he only took five steps before he turned and slowly walked back, stopping just a few feet in front of her.

"We do need a compromise, Abagail, so we both get something we want." Cade looked at the ground for a long moment before raising his gaze back to hers.

When he remained silent, Abby adjusted her spectacles and peered up at him. "What kind of compromise?"

"I know I'm not the only one concerned about you going off by yourself," Cade said. "I know Charles has talked to you about it."

"He has," Abby conceded. "And so has everyone else. I'm expecting to hear Robbie's opinion on the matter pretty soon."

A smile hovered around Cade's lips when he nodded. "You know we're telling you the truth." He quickly held up a hand. "And I know you need to see your patients."

Pleased that he didn't simply dismiss the welfare of her patients in favor of being overly cautious, Abby clasped her hands in front of her. "How do you propose I solve this small problem?"

"Your safety isn't a small problem, Abagail," Cade corrected, then looked at the ground again. "But it can be solved. I have an idea."

Now Abby smiled. Cade sounded a bit unsure. Somehow it made him more vulnerable, and she had to concentrate on not caving in to the urge to give him a hug.

"What solution do you suggest?"

Cade looked up and gave her a slightly crooked smile. "You need someone in the household who has daily assigned tasks, and can go with you whenever a patient needs you in the middle of the night."

Abby's eyebrows winged upward. She tilted her head to one side as she studied his expression. Cade certainly was serious about his solution.

"I'm assuming this person would be like Cook? A jack-of-all-trades, plus protection?" she asked.

When he nodded, her eyebrows rose even further. "And you think he should be living in my cottage with me?"

The marshal shook his head. "Not in your cottage, no."

"Well, since I have a professional reputation to keep in the community, that's good to hear," Abby said, her dry tone clearly conveying her feelings on the matter. "But having to send for someone and then wait for his arrival isn't going to work either, Cade."

"It would if he was employed in *my* household."

Abby shook her head. "It would take far too long. Even if he slept in Lillian's stable, and she's only a short walk from me, it would take too long. Besides, I'd still have to go out by myself just to rouse this person to have him trail along after me. And eventually I'd have to coax another horse out of Rayne, so he could keep up whenever I needed to travel outside of town."

"Not if you also lived in my household." Cade's gaze stayed steady on hers, but Abby could tell he was holding his breath.

Not understanding how that was a workable solution at all, Abby wrinkled her nose in thought. "Even with Geraldine there it wouldn't be proper. And I can't afford to do something improper. Which is one of the reasons I don't travel about the countryside with men in tow."

Cade looked off at a distant point and drew in a deep breath. Abby waited patiently for him to realize she was right, and that his solution wouldn't work at all.

"It would work if we were husband and wife."

"Husband and wife? Are you suggesting we get married?" Abby's eyes fairly popped out of her head. The man had lost his senses.

Cade's jaw tightened as he kept his gaze on her. The determination in his eyes told Abby he was through looking at the ground. "It's a compromise, Abagail. You can see your patients whenever you need to. When I can't go with you, our hired man will. And no one will question him living in the house with your husband there as well."

"And when my husband is off chasing bad men? What then?" Abby asked.

"Aside from our hired man going with you if necessary, your husband would be a US Marshal. Most men would think hard before putting their hands on you. And since you'd be my wife, I'd take care of any who are foolish enough to try. Word would get around. It's a good compromise, Abagail."

"How is that a compromise? I get protection and the freedom to see my patients whenever I need to, but what do you get?"

Abby shied away from stating she'd also have a husband who would likely expect certain "husbandly" rights that went along with the title. Her head was spinning. She wasn't at all sure how she felt about Cade's solution.

"A doctor for Jules."

"What?" *That* certainly wasn't what she'd expected to hear. She put her hand to her stomach and took a deep breath, willing herself to keep calm. "I don't need to be your wife to take care of Jules."

"But you're the only one who can give him a normal life," Cade countered. "You need to be there if he has another attack, not wait to be told about it the next morning. Provided my brother makes it through the night without a doctor by his side. The fact he might not scares me. So Jules would get his chance to grow into manhood, and I would get peace of mind. But the only way you can be there for him is if you're my wife. As you pointed out, you have a reputation to consider. So do I. I won't have your name sullied all over town because of me. And I don't want to run the risk of

Jules's best hope being sent home to Connecticut because your close friends and family are worried about you."

Abby reached out and steadied herself against the boards of the stall. The silence grew into a full minute. And then into another one.

She finally stood up straight, locking her spine in place as she raised her gaze to his. He held her stare as he reached up and touched his cheek. She doubted he was even aware of that particular habit of his.

"I don't know, Cade. I just don't know."

With nothing more to say, and needing time for her shocked mind to think straight again, she turned and walked toward the entrance to the barn. But that didn't stop the marshal from having the final word on the matter.

"I can make all the arrangements as soon as we get back to town, Abagail."

Chapter Eleven

Hours later, Abby sat on the front porch watching the stars. Without the soft blanket of nightly fog in San Francisco, the sky was clear and filled with bright points of light.

She'd helped Carrie settle the children back into their bedroom, since she'd moved her things into the small guest quarters set away from both the main house and the bunkhouse for the hands. The dinner dishes were washed, the floors swept, and she'd looked in on her peacefully snoring patient, who was well on the mend. With every chore she could find completed, Abby had little to do but sit on the wide front porch in the dark, watch the stars, and think.

A movement from the barn caught her eye. A tall figure carrying a shotgun in one hand and a sack in the other, strode across the yard until he disappeared around the far corner of the porch. She might have thought he hadn't noticed her sitting back in the shadows, but she easily recognized that long ground-eating stride. And nothing escaped the eagle-eyed gaze of Cade McKenzie.

Abby couldn't blame the marshal for not acknowledging her. After all, she hadn't given him an answer to what she'd privately dubbed "the bargain". But right now she was tired of thinking about it, and everything else Cade had said.

The front door swung open and Carrie stepped out onto the porch, holding tight to the shawl wrapped around her shoulders. She walked over to where Abby was sitting and took a seat beside her.

"It's a pretty night," Carrie said by way of a greeting.

"Yes, it is," Abby agreed. "The stars are beautiful."

The older woman chuckled. "Nice change from all that fog and mist in town, I suppose, though I was always partial to it. It was like walking through a gray cloud."

Abby usually felt the fog drifting through the streets at night was unnerving, but she wasn't in the mood to argue over anything, not even the weather, so she only smiled and nodded.

A few more minutes of comfortable silence passed before Carrie leaned back to rest against one of the porch posts.

"Care to tell me why you did every chore a body could do tonight? I'm surprised you didn't go out to feed the horses."

"Only because they're in the barn," Abby said before she could stop herself. "I meant I didn't feel like going out to the barn."

"I knew what you meant. It isn't the barn you're avoidin', but who's spendin' all his time in the barn. Even had Mitch bring his dinner plate out there." Carrie turned and looked at the doctor. "Wonder why he did that? He sat around in the house drinkin' his coffee for a good hour or two this mornin', and this evenin' he won't set foot inside, and you won't go out to the barn."

Abby shrugged. "He needs time to think."

"He does, or you do?" Carrie asked.

"*He* does," Abby said firmly.

"The marshal strikes me as a deliberatin' kind of thinker. What is it he needs to be thinkin' about?"

"He thinks we should get married," Abby stated, surprised at how relieved she was to say the words out loud.

Carrie coughed several times, averting her face while Abby reached over and patted her hard on the back.

"Are you all right?"

"I'm fine," Carrie got out in between coughs. "Just let me be for a minute. You go on explainin' how he came to ask you to marry him."

Abby put her hands in her lap and sighed. "He didn't ask, exactly. He only said it was a good compromise, and that's what we should do."

"Was there shenanigans goin' on last night that I don't know about?" Carrie's voice was sharp enough to cut through a piece of wood.

"Of course not," Abby instantly denied. *That* hadn't been on the marshal's mind at all. Which was part of her problem. She couldn't decide whether she was grateful for him being so gentlemanly, or insulted. But the more she sat looking at the stars, the more she was leaning toward that last one.

"What kind of compromisin' was he talkin' about?" Carrie asked.

"He'd make sure I have protection whenever I need to go out and see my patients, and he gets a doctor for his brother," Abby said. "It's more of a bargain than a marriage."

"And you aren't interested?" Carrie didn't sound convinced of that.

"Not at first. Now I don't know," Abby admitted. "I need to see my patients, but the worry is becoming a burden for everyone. To practice medicine the way I want to, and not worry everyone into an early grave, I may have to go home. And I don't want to go home. Cade is offering me a way I can stay, without being a weight to everyone I love."

"Then marry the man," Carrie said.

"It's not that simple. Once Jules is cured, I'll continue to get my protection, but Cade will be stuck with a wife. It doesn't seem like a fair bargain," Abby said.

Carrie scratched her chin. "That's what has you worried? If this bargain is fair to the marshal?"

Abby looked back up at the stars. "The man definitely needs to work on his manners, but he has strong principles. If I say 'yes', he'll have no way out of it if he has second thoughts. If I say 'no', it might hurt his pride enough for him to search for someone else to help Jules instead of allowing me to be his doctor, and I'll still be a worry to everyone."

From the corner of her eye, Abby saw her older friend roll her eyes.

"It's true. He'll either be trapped in a marriage, or I won't be allowed to help Jules," Abby said, surprised at Carrie's reaction. It should be obvious to anyone that the marshal had presented her with a difficult choice.

"I've never known why young people make everythin' so mashed up." Carrie shook her head and turned her whole body until her knees were touching Abby's. "You shouldn't be worryin' about what's fair or not. Cade McKenzie's a grown man. He can do his own thinkin' and decidin'. You just need to decide what *you* want to do. And I'll tell you the same thing I told Beth a while back. Men aren't hard to figure. They usually say what they mean, except when it comes to their feelin's. They're downright persnickity about those. You have to look for the signs on what they're really tryin' to say."

"Signs?" Fascinated, Abby stared at Carrie. "What kind of signs?"

"I'm not talking about flowers, or sweets, or baubles. But signs. Things they do, mostly. Men are more doin' than talkin'. Leastways, the good men are." Carrie added a nod at the end of her observation.

"You mean like providing for a family?" Abby asked.

"There's that," Carrie agreed. "Or like protectin' you, making sure you're safe and havin' what you want."

Abby smiled. Carrie had just described every single one of the men her friends had married. And Cook too, for that matter.

"You've got to look for the signs," the rancher's wife insisted. "Like ridin' across country because he needed to know you're safe. Or sleepin' in a chair by your bed to be sure you stay that way. And especially demandin' another man keep his hands off you." When Abby blinked, Carrie nodded again. "Or even luggin' pails of water across the yard just because you want a bath."

Carrie stood up and pulled her shawl tighter around herself. She patted Abby on her shoulder. "The marshal probably doesn't realize the signs he's givin', him bein' a man and all. He just does what he needs to do. You ponder on that. And if you want to do more talkin' on the matter, you should do it with Cade. I hear he'll be standin' guard tonight. He took the spot over near the guesthouse."

As Carrie made her way back into the house, Abby bit her lower lip and stared off into the distance. She had a lot to consider.

***

The sun was peeking over the horizon when Abby's eyes popped open. It had taken her well past midnight to get to sleep, but this morning she was rested and ready to tackle whatever the day brought. Last night she'd settled on two decisions, and one of them was that Marshal Cade McKenzie was far too used to getting his own way. It was past time he learned she could do a little arranging of things herself.

Determined to stick with the decision she'd made the night before, Abby climbed out of bed, got dressed and marched over to the ranch house. The next several hours flew by as Abby kept busy with her usual long list of things to do.

Right before sunset she returned to the guesthouse, needing time to herself. After a bath and a fresh change of clothes, she was sitting on the edge of the bed when a sharp knock sounded against the door before Carrie stuck her head around its edge.

"Are you coming into the house?" she asked.

Abby nodded but made no effort to move.

"I saw the marshal get a fresh bucket of water. I imagine he's washed up by now, so I sent Mitch over to fetch him to the house. You're goin' to have to talk to him sooner or later, and it best be sooner before the supper is spoiled."

Taking a deep breath, Abby nodded again and stood. Telling herself she only needed to put one foot in front of the other and get through the next hour, she followed Carrie out the door.

She'd barely walked through the house and stepped out onto the front porch when Mitch and Cade emerged from the barn.

***

"I'd best go check on something out back," Mitch said, drawing a puzzled glance from Cade.

"What's there to check on out back?"

Mitch rubbed his hands together. "Never you mind, it's personal. You just go on into the house."

Cade stared after the ranch hand who'd quickened his pace until he was almost running. Shaking his head at the strange behavior, Cade took three more steps toward the house before stopping in his tracks.

Abagail was standing on the porch, watching him. He figured she'd want to speak to him sooner or later. All the time he'd been riding the perimeter of the ranch he'd been working out a way to solve both their problems. And while he was sure the compromise he'd come up with would work fine, he had realized during the long hours since their talk in the barn, that he'd just sprung his whole plan on her.

I should have dropped a few hints and let her get used to the idea, Cade thought. And while he was prepared to wait a while longer for her to realize it was a good plan, he wasn't looking forward to her first saying 'no'.

He slowly climbed up to the porch, stopping on the top step when he got a good jolt as she stepped into a patch of fading sunlight. Her hair was braided with a blue ribbon entwined through it, and twisted into a fancy loop on top of her head. She stood with her hands clasped in front of her, dressed in a soft blue skirt with a wide black ribbon across her waist, topped by a snow-white blouse with lace trim on the neck and sleeves. She looked beautiful, and he could hardly breathe when she walked toward him, a soft smile on her face and a glow in her light blue eyes.

102

He opened his mouth, but when he couldn't think of a thing to say, promptly closed it again. Heat crawled through his belly when she stopped in front of him and turned her face up to his.

"I've considered what you said, Cade."

"You have?"

She inclined her head, but kept her gaze on his. "I think it's a good bargain."

"You do?"

"But I have an idea or two of my own on the whole matter."

"You what?"

Abby continued to smile at him as she backed away. "Let's talk inside."

Cade's head was spinning from what he'd just heard, so he didn't budge when she walked over to the front door.

"Are you coming?" she asked.

He managed a weak nod and finally got his feet to move. She waited a moment before disappearing into the house. Cade followed her through the door then took a quick step backwards, his back smacking against a wall. Both the ranch hands, as well as the wagon drivers and the guards, were standing at attention on one side of the room, while all the children stared back at him with big eyes, and huge smiles, from the other side. A path was open down the center, and at the other end stood the preacher, with Carrie on his right and George on his left.

Any man would recognize what was going on here and flee in terror. While Cade was still gaping at all the people in the room, he felt a light touch on his sleeve.

"Well, Marshal, have you changed your mind?"

When he saw that smug little smile and gleam of mischief in Abagail's eyes, the fog in his brain lifted away and he fought a sudden urge to grin. If his little doctor thought this shotgun wedding of hers would scare him off, she'd better think again.

Cade lifted a hand and ran one finger down the side of her cheek. When her eyes got bigger and her smile wavered, he gave in and grinned at her.

"It's a fine idea, Abagail."

Reaching for her hand, Cade drew it through the crook of his arm. He thoroughly enjoyed the stunned expression on her face as he walked her over to the preacher.

Chapter Twelve

Abby gave Carrie one, last hug. The day was exactly as she'd planned it, with the help of her friend. It might not have been the way she'd have envisioned it, if there had been any forewarning she was getting married. But even if she'd known, Abby wouldn't have been happier with a big church wedding along with the huge amount of fuss that went with planning one. Her best friends would have loved it, but she was glad to have avoided all that.

The simple setting, with the children scrubbed and present plus a handsome, although certainly not besotted, groom, suited her just fine. The only thing missing were the people she cared for the most—the four women she thought of as sisters, along with the rest of her extended family.

Well, and maybe a bit more enthusiasm from the marshal. The chaste kiss he'd placed on her cheek at the end of the ceremony was very proper. She supposed she should be happy he'd suddenly developed some manners.

Even though the hour was getting late, Abby would have lingered. Only because her planning hadn't extended beyond the wedding itself. She had no idea what to expect next. From the corner of her eye, she'd caught Cade stifling a yawn. Knowing how little sleep he'd managed after spending the entire night before on guard duty, she thought she'd best make a final check on George before retiring to the guesthouse. She'd have to wait and see if Cade intended to join her there, for the sake of appearances if nothing else, or take up his solitary bed in the barn.

"I should look in on George."

Abby blinked when Carrie shook her head.

"I already checked on him and he's fine. Sleepin' and snorin' away as usual. You go on with your husband, now."

Carrie leaned over and whispered in Abby's ear. "It'll be fine. Don't you worry none."

With heat blooming along her cheeks, Abby managed a weak smile. "Well. Good night, then. And thank you for everything. It was wonderful."

A sheen of tears welled up in Carrie's eyes as she held Abby at arm's length. "A woman should be able to plan this day to her likin'. And she shouldn't be forced to go along with other people's notions unless she's good and ready."

Carrie had turned her head and raised her voice loud enough for Cade to hear. Abby thought her whole face must look like it was on fire. There was no mistaking what Carrie was talking about. It got worse when she peeked over at Cade. He simply lifted one eyebrow and held out his hand.

"Your patient's in good hands. We should let everyone get some rest, Mrs. McKenzie," he said.

Left with little choice, Abby placed her hand in his and walked with him out into the night. They crossed the wide porch together. When Cade dropped her hand and descended the steps, she stood on the edge of the porch and looked up to the sky. The stars seemed closer and brighter tonight than ever, and she took comfort in that. She'd always considered it a miracle to be surrounded by so much beauty.

"Abagail?"

Cade was standing below her, his arms outstretched. In the next second he'd lifted her off her feet, holding her aloft for several seconds before carefully setting her on the ground beside him. While she was still breathless from the easy display of her husband's strength, he took her hand in his again and started toward the back of the ranch house. They walked together in silence until they reached the door of the guesthouse. Abby stopped by Cade's side and looked up at him. He smiled and pushed open the door before stepping aside for her to enter first.

Deciding the man probably didn't even know any of the romantic gestures that went with a wedding, even if he had been inclined to practice one or two of them, Abby stepped inside.

The room was spacious and decorated in muted colors of greens and browns. A stove for heat occupied one corner, and the opposite corner had a large tub, table and ornate screens which could be pulled together for privacy. A huge bed dominated the center of the room. It was big enough for three or four people, with a multi-colored quilt as a cover, and a thick comforter folded across the end.

"Very nice," Cade said.

His new wife smiled. "It is, isn't it? And it suits Lillian."

"This is her room?"

Abby nodded. "Yes, although we all use it when we're here. Charles brought the bigger bed from town, and Beth had this lovely quilt made just for this room." She walked over and touched it before turning her gaze back to Cade.

"All your friends and their husbands have stayed here?" he asked, eyeing the bed.

"They have," Abby laughed. "This is where Beth and John spent their wedding night."

She didn't add that it was a day sooner than the ceremony, but considering they were almost killed by a hired bounty hunter, Abby thought they were entitled to a little leeway in the matter. But she wasn't sure what Cade would make of the story, and didn't want him thinking the worst about her family.

All of them had faced hard choices, and more than a few very frightening events, and had survived to find love and happiness with each other. They didn't deserve to be poorly judged.

No. She'd wait to tell him the stories after he'd been around them for a while, like maybe a year or two.

"What do you know about wedding nights?" Cade asked.

Abby gave him a surprised look. "I'm a doctor. I can assure you I know all about wedding nights."

Cade frowned. "You're telling me that everything you know you got from one of your medical books?"

"Medical books are very thorough, Marshal McKenzie. And very detailed," Abby said, doing her best to sound as if she wasn't the least embarrassed by the subject. After all, she'd discussed anatomy with her male colleague, Dr. Melton, and at times her patients, when necessary.

"Uh huh." Cade looked around then glanced over at Abby. "We'll be comfortable here for the night. And just so you won't have to consult any books, sleeping is all we'll be doing."

Abby went still while she absorbed the meaning of his words. It seemed there was another wedding night tradition the marshal had no intention of following. Tamping down a sharp, unexpected feeling of disappointment, Abby merely nodded. Determined to be as blunt and matter-of-fact as he was, she looked at the bed.

"As you have repeatedly reminded me, you're much bigger than I am, so I'll be happy to give the bed to you, Marshal McKenzie. I'm sure I'll be comfortable sleeping in the chair. After all, I am used to that sort of thing whenever I visit a sick patient."

"There's a couple of things we need to talk about, Abagail." Cade said. "You won't be visiting patients by yourself anymore, and you won't be sleeping in that chair when there's a decent bed available." He walked over and stood next to her, reaching down to lightly bounce one hand on top of the quilt. "It's big enough for both of us to sleep on and not bother each other."

"Not bother each other," Abby echoed. When Cade looked over at her, she forced herself to smile back at him. "Of course. I take it this means you won't be standing guard tonight?"

"I'm a light sleeper. Learned that in the army and it's stuck with me. Nothing will get near us if that has you worried." He paused and looked out the single window nearest the door.

"We need to leave at first light. I have to organize the men to hunt down Linder, and you have Jules to see to. I'll keep most of the guards here, but a couple will come back with us."

A sinking feeling rolled through Abby's stomach. Of course he expected her to keep her end of the bargain, and she was indeed anxious to check on Jules. But it was harder than she'd imagined accepting it was the only reason he'd married her.

She jerked slightly when he lifted her chin with one finger until their eyes met, then gently cradled the side of her face in his hand. "You get ready for bed. I'm going to wash up. I'll be back in half an hour."

While Abby was still staring at him with her mouth half open, he turned and headed out the door.

***

Several hours later Cade lay awake, listening to his wife's soft breathing. He wasn't surprised at how much he liked having her near. He would have liked a wedding night even more, but he'd be damned if the first time he made love to his wife was in the same bed used by another man.

He could wait. Which is one of the reasons he'd kept his hands off her. If he hadn't, there wouldn't be any waiting. Since he was sure she'd never been with a man, he didn't want her first experience to be the way it was described in a medical book.

There was also the bargain. He knew why Abagail had married him, and he intended to live up to his part and keep her safe. And he was certain she'd do her very best for his younger brother. He thought he'd be fine with that, but now he was having a lot more than just second thoughts on the matter. And her coming to their marriage bed out of duty didn't sit right with him.

A man could want more than that.

Cade looked out the window, gauging the number of hours left until dawn. He no sooner decided he should try to sleep when he was distracted by a soft sound from Abagail, followed by a distinct shiver. He gingerly reached out and touched her arm, surprised at how cool she felt. He was about to pull the comforter up, thinking to tuck it around her, when she suddenly rolled and plastered herself against his side.

Not sure how to get the comforter around her without waking her, Cade had the decision made for him when she threw a slender arm over his chest. He carefully eased her head onto his shoulder and settled her more comfortably against him, gritting his teeth when she wiggled to get closer.

Her breath stirred against his chest. "I like the stars."

He tilted his chin down to look at her face. She was still sleeping. Smiling, Cade curled an arm around her waist.

"I do too," he whispered, dropping a soft kiss into her hair. She smelled like lemon and sunshine.

Still smiling, he closed his eyes and dropped into sleep.

Chapter Thirteen

"I don't know, Ben. Maybe we shouldn'a shot that ranch man."

Ben Linder looked up from the gun he was carefully cleaning.

"You're the one who shot him, Tommy. Little late to be complainin' now."

Ben went back to cleaning the gun. It used to belong to his cousin, Frank. The two of them had fled Nebraska together, leaving the sod huts and long, backbreaking work of farming an unforgiving prairie to their parents and siblings. But Frank didn't need the gun anymore. Ben had taken it out of his cousin's lifeless hands when they'd been caught in a gunfight with a posse of Marshal Noriega's men, led by that new marshal from Chicago.

"I didn't mean to shoot that ranch man, but he was goin' for his gun." The short, slightly built Tommy, who was still a year shy of twenty, stuck his thumbs into the top of his belt buckle. "You saw him."

The whine in his tone set Ben's teeth on edge. "It's done. No reason to fret over it."

"We don't know that," came a voice from across the campfire.

One of the newer members of the gang stood up. With his black hair, dark eyes and homely, irregular features, Hal was the one usually mistaken for Ben's kin instead of the blond, womanizing Frank. While the two cousins may have been opposite in looks, in almost everything else they were the same side of the coin.

"Frank shot the wrong man when we robbed that supply train. He set those US Marshals on our trail." Hal had never bothered to hide the fact he'd never liked Frank much.

Ben stopped polishing the barrel of his cousin's prized gun and set it on the ground beside him.

"We had no way of knowin' a federal judge was hitchin' a ride on that supply wagon. We thought the extra guards were on account of the load of gold coins in that wagon. Not to protect no judge."

Hal shrugged. "Frank shouldn'a opened fire so quick. He always was too trigger happy."

"And he paid a price for it," Ben snapped back. "He's dead. McKenzie and Noriega got their judge-killer, so they have no reason to be chasin' us any longer." Ben looked around the campfire at the other three members of the gang, who were holding ignored plates of food and listening intently. "And there aren't any US Marshals in San Francisco."

When grunts echoed around the campfire, Ben picked up the gun again. "The pickin's here are good. Better than robbin' those rancheros around Los Angeles. Plenty of gamblers and miners in this town stumblin' around drunk, with their pockets full of gold dust. Same for the ones travelin' on the road from the gold fields in the mountains. It's easy money. If we leave, where are we goin'? There's a lot of mountains to the east and north, and winter will be hittin' them soon enough. If you want to spend the next six months ridin' through that kind of cold and snow, then you just go ahead and take off."

There was a restless stirring as looks were exchanged all around. Hal sat again, but his chin jutted out as he continued to glare at the gang's leader.

"I heard some rumors last time I was in town. Rumors about a marshal. If Tommy shot the wrong man like Frank did, we could be in a whole lot of trouble."

Complete silence settled on the group as all eyes were fixed on Ben. He slowly met each gaze, staring until the man looked away. He saved Hal for last.

"Maybe I should take a ride into town and hang about for a few days. See if I can hear those same rumors." He looked directly at the dark-haired man who kept challenging him. "Maybe you ought to come with me. Make sure I don't miss anything."

And to keep you from talking the men into taking off while I'm gone, Ben thought. Better to have Hal where he could keep an eye on the troublemaker.

Frank and his cousin had shared a lot, but not everything. Frank might have been blessed with the pretty face, but Ben had gotten the brains.

Chapter Fourteen

Cade stretched out his long frame before he opened his eyes. The first thing he noticed was the empty space beside him. Thinking Abagail must have moved to the far side of the bed, he turned his head in that direction. After opening one eye, the other quickly followed when he only saw mattress and no wife. And a lot more light coming into the room than there should have been at dawn.

He sat straight up and stared out the window. He didn't need to walk outside to know it was full-on morning. Swinging his long legs over the edge of the bed, he crossed to the chair where he'd left his clothes the night before. Once he had his pants on, Cade dealt with his socks and boots, all the while shaking his head. He hadn't slept this late since he was a kid, and certainly not after he'd joined the army.

And right there was another bit of astonishment. He hadn't heard a damn thing when Abagail left the bed, got dressed and exited the room. He wasn't sure how he felt about that. Or how she'd accomplished such an unbelievable feat. But he meant to find out.

Tucking his shirt into his pants, he slapped his belt into place before grabbing his hat and striding out the door. Thinking Abagail was likely in the main house, he took the back steps leading into the kitchen. Several of the older girls were at the table, peeling more vegetables. The oldest one had sparkling green eyes and gave him a bright, generous smile.

"Morning, Marshal. Are you looking for Doctor Abby?" Her mouth twitched at the corners. "I mean, your wife?"

Cade's first inclination was to keep going into the main part of the house, but knowing that might be taken as rude and hurt the girl's feelings, he stopped. He stood silent for a moment, not sure what to say. Except for Jules, he didn't have much experience with kids. Most of them, especially the females, tended to take one look at his scar and scamper off in the other direction. But this girl was still watching him and smiling.

"Do you know where she is?" he finally asked.

"She helped make breakfast and then went to see Mister George."

Cade nodded his thanks. "I appreciate it, um…"

"Kathy. It's short for Kathleen. It was my mama's name, too."

Belatedly remembering his hat, Cade snatched it off his head and smiled back at her. "Thank you, Kathleen."

He strode out the door as Kathy and her friends burst into giggles and excited whispers.

Thinking females got an early start on that peculiar behavior, Cade looked around. He spotted Carrie sitting alone at the table, holding a tin mug in both her hands.

She grinned as Cade crossed the room. Pushing herself out of her chair, she took another cup down from the shelf next to the sink. Filling it from the steaming pot on the stove, Carrie walked back and handed it to him before sitting and picking up her own mug again.

"Lookin' for your wife?"

Cade nodded and took a gulp of the coffee. He closed his eyes against the sudden growl in his stomach, sorry there wasn't enough time to eat. But they had to leave if they were going to make it back to town before midnight. And he still had to get the horses ready, and most likely would have to coax Abagail into hurrying with whatever she insisted on toting along with them. If they left too much later, they might end up spending the night on the trail. With the Linder gang still wandering about, he did not want to do that. Especially since Abagail would get caught in the middle of a fight.

Thinking he might take more than the extra man or two he'd been planning on, Cade set the cup on the table. He glanced over at the open bedroom door.

"Is Abagail in with George?"

"Nope. George is sittin' on the front porch." Carrie looked toward the window. "I'm keepin' my eye on him to be sure he stays there and doesn't go wanderin' about."

She got up and went to the stove. Picking up a large spoon in one hand and a plate with the other, she started shifting the contents of a frying pan onto the plate. Carrie set the mound of food on the table and pushed it over to Cade.

"Your wife said to feed you and then send you on out to get the rest of your things packed. She's seein' to the horses."

Cade's gaze bounced from Carrie to the plate of food and then back again. "*She's* seeing to the horses?"

Lifting up her coffee mug, Carrie grinned back at him. "She is. Said you were tuckered out and needed to sleep. It bein' such a hard ride back to town and all." She nodded and took a sip of her coffee. "Yep. That's what your wife said." Carrie stared at him for a long moment. "I'm bettin' you know a lot more about keepin' the law than you do about women, Marshal McKenzie. So I'm goin' to give you good advice."

Cade raised an eyebrow but remained silent.

"You've chased Abby, made sure she's safe, and I can see how you look at her. Also noticed you came up with a reason she should marry you quick enough. Those are fine traits in a man. But a woman likes a little romance."

Uncomfortable, Cade shifted his weight from one foot to the other. "Is that right."

"That's all I have to say on the matter." Carrie pointed to the chair in front of him. "You best sit and eat. Your wife said you should, and she's a doctor. We always do what Doctor Abby tells us. She's a real good doctor."

He might not know much about romance, but he certainly knew how to run his own life, and it seemed his wife, *the doctor*, was still arranging things.

We're going to have to have a little talk about that, Cade thought. But he admitted to himself that Abagail was right when she said it was a long ride. And he *was* hungry. Choosing practical over pride, Cade sat, ignoring the soft chuckle from Carrie. Placing his hat next to his plate, he took the fork she handed him and dug in.

***

Twenty minutes later, Cade pushed back from the table. Thanking Carrie for the meal, he grabbed his hat and headed out the door.

When Mitch touched her arm, Abby looked up. The old ranch hand jerked his head toward the house. She lifted a hand to shade her eyes, but didn't need more than a glance to know Cade was awake and coming in her direction. She turned back to Marron and gave his neck a hard pat. As if he realized something was up, her horse swiveled his head around and stared at her. She took a deep breath and wrinkled her nose at the animal.

"Don't give me that look. The marshal is very levelheaded. I'm sure he'll be fine with, well, everything."

"Where's Abagail?"

Abby froze at the sound of the deep voice directly behind her.

Mitch cleared his throat several times before finally saying, "she's right here." Abby closed her eyes at the sound of the ranch hand walking away.

"You may as well turn around," Cade said.

Stiffening her spine, Abby turned, lifting her chin so she could look up at Cade from beneath her broad-brimmed hat.

He crossed his arms over his chest and took a slow, long once-over, from her head to her toes and then back up again.

"I suppose you have a reason for dressing like a boy?"

She didn't care much for the disapproval she heard in his voice. Lifting her chin just a notch higher, she refused to look away. "Have you ever ridden in a skirt, Marshal McKenzie?"

He held her stare for a long moment before his eyes crinkled at the corners. "Can't say that I have, Dr. McKenzie."

Abby blinked at the name before taking a deep breath and getting back to the subject at hand. "Well, even in one made especially for riding, it flaps around your legs, and that extra material makes it more difficult to mount or dismount. Especially if you're in a hurry. These clothes are much more practical."

Cade took another slow look, then nodded. "I can see the reasoning of that."

"Oh." Expecting more of an argument, Abby quickly deflated. "Well, then. Since we're in agreement, Mitch went to saddle your horse. How long will it take to pack your things?"

"Hold on, a minute, Abagail," Cade said. "Who told you to dress like a boy? Because I'm sure you didn't learn that from your family back East."

Startled by the question, Abby's eyes opened wide, magnified by her spectacles. "Lillian did. She and Beth always wear britches when they ride to the ranch. And of course, so does Rayne, whenever she can get away and come into town. Maggie doesn't care to ride on her own, so she travels in the wagon with Ian when she visits Rayne's or Lillian's ranch."

"Is that right," Cade said. "And how did you learn to move so quietly?"

Abby's forehead wrinkled slightly. "I don't know what you're talking about."

He took a step closer and wrapped both hands gently around her upper arms. "You got up, got dressed and left our room this morning, and I didn't hear you. That hasn't happened since the last time I had too much to drink."

She suddenly smiled. "And when was that?"

"Not last night," Cade responded, then grinned back at her. "The night before I left home and joined the army. That was ten years ago, so don't get your hopes up it will happen again any time soon."

"That's good to know," Abby said, meaning it. She'd seen far too much abuse of the human body because of liquor. "We need to be on our way before it gets any later. I'm anxious to check on Jules, and my other patients."

"Abagail."

She raised an eyebrow at him.

Cade raised one of his own right back at her. "How did you learn to move so quietly?"

Resigned that there was another thing Marshal McKenzie would have to get used to, Abby sighed. "From Master Kwan."

"Master Kwan," Cade repeated. "Who is Master Kwan?"

When she hesitated, his hands tightened slightly on her arms.

"We'll stand here the rest of the day, if that's what you want," Cade said.

"He's a good friend of Lillian's. He teaches all of us different ways we can protect ourselves." Abby stopped, searching for a way to explain the Chinese man to her husband without him having a fit.

"Different ways? You mean like that Chinese way of fighting with your hands?" The disbelief in Cade's voice had Abby flinching inside.

She just knew he wasn't going to like this.

"This Master Kwan is teaching you how to fight with your bare hands?" Cade repeated, staring at her as if she'd grown two heads.

She reached up and patted his cheek. "Not fight. Protect ourselves long enough to get away. That's what Master Kwan always says. Run away if you can."

"Wouldn't it be more practical for him to teach you how to shoot?" Cade asked.

At least he didn't sound angry, which Abby took as a good sign. "Oh, Master Kwan doesn't own a gun. Beth gives us lessons in shooting. Rayne too, when she's in town."

"Beth. Uh huh." Cade dropped his arms and rolled his eyes heavenward. "I can see we'll have a lot to talk about on our ride home, Abagail. I'll go grab my gear."

He took three long steps before turning around to face her again. "We'll start by me explaining why you can't arrange everything."

Before she could think of anything to say, he'd crossed the rest of the yard and disappeared into the barn.

Abby reached for Marron's reins and gently pulled the big stallion's head down to give him a hard scratch between the ears. Staring into those liquid brown eyes she shook her head.

"I have no idea what the man is talking about."

Chapter Fifteen

They reached Cade's home late in the evening, circling around the front to head for the small stable at the back of the house. Cade dismounted then walked over to give Abby a hand down from the chocolate-brown stallion she called Marron.

She'd surprised him with how well she'd handled the big, high-spirited horse. But he still added working in a few riding instructions to his growing mental list of things he needed to do, now that he had a wife to look after.

He also just plain liked spending time with her. He enjoyed her company. She didn't talk too much, or expect him to keep up a constant chatter, either. She took long hours in the saddle without complaint, and didn't ask him to stop and collect her hairpins every time one popped out of the coil at the nape of her neck. Halfway home she'd given up and pulled a narrow ribbon out of her saddlebag, using it to tie her hair and let it hang in one glorious fall down her back.

Cade admired it for the rest of the ride. He also liked the feminine curve of her back, and the way her pretty little behind fit in the saddle.

Abby was down and stretching before he reached her. Disappointed at missing a chance to put his hands on his wife, Cade tried not to gape when her movements stretched her cotton shirt tight over her breasts. He abruptly turned away as heat curled inside him. A sensation he'd been living with ever since she'd rolled up against him the night before.

He walked back to his own mount and briefly leaned his forehead against the saddle.

"Are you all right?"

His wife's voice was just behind him. When he shifted around to face her, she brought a hand up and laid it against his scarred cheek. It took every ounce of self-discipline for him to keep from leaning over and kissing her then and there.

There was no doubt about it. He badly wanted to take his wife to bed and show her what wasn't in those medical books of hers. The fact he had every right to do just that wasn't making it any easier on him. But he needed her to want him too. Nothing could be better than Abagail, soft and willing, beneath him.

Of course, it wasn't against his principles to help her get to that point.

"You do feel a little hot. You should lie down." Abby nodded as if the matter were settled.

Cade decided it was time to show his take-charge wife that he could do a little arranging of his own. He reached up and lifted her hand from his cheek, raised it to his lips and placed a soft kiss into the center of her palm.

Her quick, indrawn breath added fuel to the fire in his belly. Letting instinct take over, Cade bent down and claimed her mouth with his. His intent was to give her a gentle brush of his lips, but that thought fled as fast as it formed. When Abagail's mouth softened and opened under his, he deepened the kiss, his tongue searching out the warmth there. When her hands slid up his chest, Cade's arms came around her, tightening his hold until she was molded to his chest, and every exquisite curve imprinted on his brain.

When he realized he was backing her toward a loose pile of hay, Cade lifted his head and took several, heaving breaths.

"Cade? Is something wrong?"

Abagail's voice pulled his straying thoughts back into place. Taking another deep breath, Cade looked at her with a crooked smile.

"Nothing's wrong. We'd better see to the horses." He dropped his arms and stepped back, but couldn't resist a quick kiss when she kept staring at him.

"Let's get you into the house, Mrs. McKenzie."

She nodded but turned back when Cade reached for her hand.

"You take the bridles, Abagail. I'll get the saddles." He grinned at her. "Remember those medical books telling you who's bigger and stronger?"

He was still grinning when she rolled her eyes at him, but turned to remove the bridle and bit. He'd never stripped the tack off horses, and got the animals properly put away and fed, so fast. Abby picked up her medical bag before they left the stables for the short walk to the back of his house.

Carrie's words echoed in his head just as they reached the bottom step leading to the kitchen door. Maybe a little romance wasn't a bad idea. Might even help matters along.

Without any warning he bent over, and in one fluid motion picked up his wife. She quickly wrapped her free arm around his neck.

"What are you doing?"

Abagail's breath whispered past his ear as he adjusted his hold on her. "I'm carrying you into your new home. Isn't that the way the tradition goes?"

He popped open the door with his foot and swept them inside to the sound of her laughter.

"Good heavens."

Cade stopped dead in his tracks at hearing the unexpected voice. It hadn't occurred to him his cousin might still be up and puttering around the kitchen. But there she was, sitting at the small table, a cup of tea in her hand. Steaming mugs were also in front of Cook and John Davis. All three turned at the same time and gaped at the intruders.

The drawn-out silence was broken when Cook slapped the palm of his hand onto the table with a hard thump. "I see you found Abby."

Geraldine jumped to her feet. "Is Doctor Abby hurt?"

Barely masking his annoyance with a fixed smile, Cade shook his head while he set Abagail on her feet. Biting her bottom lip, his wife quickly crossed the small space and set her medical bag on the table.

"We're glad to be here, at last," Abby said with a note of cheer in her voice. "Everything is fine at the ranch. George is recovering nicely and the children are healthy. I'd like to hear how Jules is doing on his restricted eating? I need to make a proper record of everything he eats, and any more breathing attacks."

Cade crossed his arms over his chest. Judging by the frowns on their faces, Abby wasn't distracting her audience at all with her medical talk, and he wasn't surprised at the sideways glance John sent his way. Cade expected he'd be explaining himself to the men in her family. Starting with the two sitting at his kitchen table.

Geraldine grabbed onto Abby's arm. "Jules is fine. Better than fine as a matter of fact. We can talk about him later. I want to know why Cade was carrying you, and why in heaven's name are you dressed like that?"

Taking issue with her demanding tone of voice toward his wife, Cade narrowed his gaze on his cousin.

"It's a long ride. Too long to make in a skirt. We all wear britches when we ride." Abby looked at John. "Don't we?"

John shrugged, drawing a frown from Abby and a snort from Cook.

The tall gangly man who'd raised Lillian for years and considered her, and all her friends, as his parental responsibility, looked from Cade to Abby. "You need to answer Dina's question. And not about how you're dressed."

Now the marshal did some staring of his own at the man's casual use of his cousin's childhood nickname.

"Well," Abby started, casting a quick glance over her shoulder at her husband. "Cade caught up with me at the ranch."

When she paused, Cook leaned forward. "Did the marshal do any more catching?"

As Abby stammered and turned red, Cade had had enough. Not even a stand-in father was allowed to embarrass his wife. He walked over and put his hands on her shoulders.

"We're married."

Geraldine let out a soft, "oh, my", and quickly lowered herself into a chair. John pursed his lips and looked up at the ceiling, while Cook continued to stare at the marshal.

"Dina, you and Abby take that teapot and a couple of cups and go into the parlor," Cook said.

"I don't think I should be banished to the parlor while you're discussing my life," Abby said, the softness in her voice taking away the sting of her words.

Cade leaned down and whispered into her ear. "They have a right to an explanation, Abagail. I'd appreciate it if you would find out how Jules is doing?" Knowing mentioning her patient would sway his wife, Cade gave her shoulders a light squeeze when she nodded.

The men were silent while the women left, with Abby clearly dragging her feet. Once the kitchen door closed behind them, John leaned back in his chair and shook his head at Cade.

"My wife is not going to be happy when I tell her Abby is married."

Aware that both Davis and Jamison had Luke Donovan in mind to be Abagail's husband, Cade set his feet apart and stared at the man. They would all just have to accept Abagail being married to him.

"Did you have to get married at the point of George Cowan's shotgun?" Cook asked.

"Or Carrie's?" John added, the corners of his mouth curling upward.

With an effort, Cade held onto his temper. "No."

"Then why the rush?" John asked.

Cade switched his attention to the investigator. "We had our reasons."

"The girl wasn't forced to get married?" Cook asked. He didn't even blink at Cade's blistering glare.

"I don't force women."

The tension in the room thickened. Cade's jaw tightened as he faced the two men. A full minute ticked by on the old clock hanging near a cupboard before Cook's shoulders visibly relaxed, and John grinned.

"Did Abby force *you*?"

A bark of laughter escaped before Cade could stop it. Even Cook chuckled at John's dry question.

"She does likes to arrange things. She let me know we were getting married when she took me to stand in front of a preacher." Cade reached a hand up and touched the scar on his face. "Had everyone assembled and even a supper laid out."

John laughed. "Sounds like Abby. Also explains why there's no ring on her finger."

Cade shrugged. "I'll take care of that tomorrow."

"The best advice I can give you is make sure you pay attention to those kinds of details in a marriage. Women have ways of letting you know when you should have paid more attention to things. Especially our women," John said.

"I haven't heard her complain," Cade countered.

John grinned. "They don't complain, Marshal. They get all the others to gang up on you until you fix whatever it is they aren't complaining about."

Cook grunted and pushed away from the table. He went to the stove, lifted the coffee pot, and poured out a large mug before returning to his seat. Setting the mug down in front of the empty chair on his right, he looked up at Cade.

"Sit and tell us what George said about the men who shot him."

***

"We have to plan a proper dinner party, and have all your friends over to celebrate your marriage."

Abby smiled at Geraldine's enthusiasm, grateful for the suggestion. Until this moment, she hadn't thought about how everyone would react to her sudden wedding, other than being disappointed they weren't there to see it. Or that they'd hoped she'd marry Luke.

Maybe she should have told Cade they needed to wait until they returned to town. But who knows how long it would have taken to talk her family into accepting her decision, and then go about arranging a wedding? And she wouldn't have been able to stay close to Jules, and still would have remained a constant worry to her loved ones every time she set foot out the door to see a patient.

"Tell me how he asked you to marry him? Did he get down on one knee like a proper gentleman?"

"No, he didn't," Abby laughed. "But then we were in a barn at the time."

"A barn?" Geraldine put a hand to her throat and gasped. "He proposed to you in a barn?"

"It wasn't a proposal, exactly," Abby confessed.

"Did he order you to marry him? That would be so like Cade," Geraldine declared.

"No." Abby shook her head and thought it over as she took a sip of tea. "It was more of an explanation." Satisfied with that word, Abby smiled at Geraldine.

"What did he explain to you?"

"That I needed help to stay safe when I went to visit my patients, and he needed help with Jules."

"Help?" Geraldine put her hands on her hips and her jaw dropped open. "That was his proposal? Bartering as if you were at the market stalls?"

Thinking she wasn't going about this right, Abby tried again. "In a manner of speaking. But it's a very good arrangement for both of us."

"That's what you want out of this marriage? An arrangement?" Geraldine asked, watching Abby closely.

Within a heartbeat Abby could still feel the strength of Cade's arms around her, and the warmth of his lips on hers. She ducked her head at the sudden burst of heat on her face.

"I haven't had a chance to mention that I've met Lillian, Beth and Maggie, as well as their husbands." Geraldine nodded when Abby's head snapped up. "They were kind enough to stop by and stay for tea while you and Cade were gone. I can tell you that they'll see right through this 'arrangement' nonsense, the same way I am. And until they get here, it's up to me to be sure my brick-headed cousin sees how stupid he's being."

"Geraldine, I'm sure Cade and I will..." Abby sat back when the older woman waved her hands.

"Dina. You must call me Dina. All my close friends and family do."

"I'd like that very much," Abby smiled. "But you must realize that Cade and I can..."

She was cut off again when Geraldine suddenly put one finger to her mouth.

"Shhh. Here they come. You leave this to me."

Abby frowned. "Leave what to you?"

When the three men stepped into the parlor, Geraldine rose and tugged on Abby's sleeve until the younger woman stood beside her.

"Cade, it's very late, and Abby is exhausted. I think it's best if we go on up to bed."

"I was planning on that," Cade said, his gaze on Abby. "John and Cook are just leaving."

"All right. Since your bedroom only has that small cot in it, and Jules needs his sleep so we can't disturb him, Abby can share my room." She smiled at Abby. "I have a very nice, fourposter bed I brought with me all the way from Chicago. I'm sure we'll be quite comfortable."

Before another word could be said, she locked one arm through Abby's and marched her right past a speechless Cade and grinning John.

The marshal was still staring after the two women when they disappeared up the stairs.

"Your plans for the evening suddenly change?" John asked.

Cade turned a hot glare on the investigator, who only grinned. Cook gave them both a bland look before heading out the front door.

"Now all you have to do is figure out what you need to fix," John continued, grinning as he clapped a hand on Cade's broad shoulder. "Welcome to the family, Marshal McKenzie."

Chapter Sixteen

The hallway clock chimed nine times as Abby descended the stairs the following morning, still randomly sticking pins into her hair to keep it in place. She had no doubt the whole coil was listing to one side, but there wasn't time to fix it now. Abby shoved a last pin into the tangled mess and put it out of her mind.

She peeked into the front parlor, but it was empty, so she continued on to the kitchen. Muffled voices floated down the hall. She recognized Cade's deep tones and the higher, more excited ones of his brother. Not sure of the reception she'd get from the young boy, she paused outside the kitchen and took a quick breath. Telling herself she'd faced much more difficult things than a pouting or even angry child, Abby put a smile on her face and pushed open the door.

Her gaze went directly to Cade. "Good morning."

The words were barely out of her mouth before Jules jumped out of his chair and hurtled across the room, coming close to knocking Abby over when he threw his arms around her waist.

"You and Cade are really married?" He looked up at her with shining eyes. "He's not funning with me, is he?"

Abby ran a gentle hand over his hair and smiled at his upturned face. "No, he's not."

Jules gave a small whoop and grabbed her hand, tugging her over to the table. "You can have my chair. I feel fine, and now you'll be living here so I'll always feel fine, won't I?"

Cade stood up and placed a hand on top of his brother's head, effectively stopping his jumping up and down. "Behave, Jules. You sit and finish that broth. Abagail will use my chair until I get another one."

"You have to give her your chair because she's your wife," Jules declared. He slid into his seat and picked up his spoon.

Cade looked at Abby and winked. "You sit here. I have it on the best authority I *have* to give you my chair."

Laughing, Abby sat and folded her hands on the table. "I'm glad you're awake, Jules. There's something I want to talk to you about."

The boy's shoulders slumped, and he kept his gaze on his soup bowl. "Are you going to tell me I'm supposed to stay in bed?"

"No, I'm not," Abby assured him. "As long as you're feeling fine, you should be up and moving around. It will help you get better."

Jules looked up and grinned at her. "Can I go with Dina to see Mister Cook? He said I could come and visit Ammie, if you said it was all right."

"Well. Let's bargain a bit."

Dina gave a loud sniff from where she stood, stirring a pot on the stove. "Jules, if you need help understanding what a bargain is, Cade can explain it to you."

Abby's hand covered her smile and she peeked over her fingers at Cade. The tic in the marshal's jaw was back.

"Dina." He only said the one word, but it was enough for his cousin to shrug and turn back to her boiling pot.

Turning her full attention to Jules, Abby considered him for a moment. "Do you know what a promise is?"

"Of course I do," Jules said. "I'm not a baby."

"That's good. Then you know if you make a promise, you have to keep it?"

When he nodded again, Abby did the same. "All right. I promise you can go to see Ammie today. But only if you promise to eat what Cook gives you and nothing else, and if you feel sickly, you'll tell him right away. Can you do that?"

Jules set his spoon down and laid his hand over his heart. "I promise, Doctor Abby."

She leaned over and patted his arm. "Then we have a bargain. I also need to tell you that I can't promise you'll always feel well just because I'm living here now. But I'll do my best to see that you do."

"All right," Jules nodded.

"You made a fine bargain, Jules." Cade smiled at his brother. "Abagail? I need to talk with you, in private, for a moment."

Abby rose, surprised when Cade took her hand and walked beside her to the front parlor. Once inside he closed the door, turned and swept an arm around her. Lowering his head, he thoroughly kissed her until she could hardly catch her breath.

When he stepped back, she stared at him, her eyes huge behind her spectacles. He bent over and picked hairpins off the floor, holding them out to her with a grin. Abby reached a hand to the back of her head just as what remained of her coil fell, and waves of hair cascaded around her shoulders. Thoroughly exasperated, she gathered it up and worked it into another coil, snatching pins out of Cade's outstretched hand. Thankfully, he didn't say a word about her failure to tame her unruly hair.

When she'd managed to anchor it back into place, she turned to her husband. "What did you want to talk about?"

Cade looked away for a moment. "Do you know what's wrong with Jules?"

Since she could hear the worry in his voice, she waited until his gaze returned to her. "I'm not sure. But I have an idea. I still need to read over the notes I wrote after the first time I was here, and finish consulting my medical books. I also want to discuss my suspicions with Dr. Melton."

Cade nodded. "I'm going to hire a suitable man to look after the horses and work around the house. He can stay in the spare room in the stable and go with you when you visit your patients, whenever I'm not here."

He paused and touched the scar on the side of his face. "I keep my promises, too."

Abby wasn't too sure she liked her new husband taking charge of her life, but she didn't have time to discuss it this morning. "All right," Abby said. "I need to stop by my house and pack some clothes and books."

"I'll take you. Then I'll see you this afternoon. I have a few details to take care of today, and I need to check with the men I've hired to help track Ben Linder." Cade leaned down and gave her a quick, hard kiss. "And I'm going to buy a proper bed."

Leaving her with that thought, Cade headed for the door. Abby stood where she was, listening to his footsteps echo across the porch and then fade away.

***

An hour later, while Dina was upstairs getting an excited Jules ready for his visit, Abby answered a loud knock on the front door.

She squealed with surprise when all her friends, including Rayne, stood crowding the portal and beaming back at her.

Lillian stepped forward first and gave her cousin a long hug. "Welcome home."

The others followed suit amid excited greetings, which drew both Geraldine and Jules down the stairs.

While Dina instantly joined the happy confusion, Jules, in the grand tradition of males everywhere, simply eyed the swirl of skirts, kisses and hugs, before turning tail and bounding back up the stairs.

Maggie grinned. "Now that's a smart lad you have there. Did exactly what my Ian would have done."

"And has done, on many occasions," Lillian put in.

"He told me himself, he did, that he'd rather be beaten with his hammer than get caught in the middle of one of our lady talks," Maggie laughed.

"Tremain gives thanks daily that we live out far enough he rarely has to face all of us at once. He still shudders over the last time he did," Rayne said.

"Speaking of 'lady talks'," I do believe it's precisely why we're here. And the main topic today will be marriage." Beth gave a pointed look at Abby, who groaned out loud.

"Maybe we should talk about babies? It's a much happier subject," Abby said.

Now that she was faced with having to answer all the questions that were sure to come her way, she really, really wished she'd told Cade the marriage had to wait. Or they'd kept the news of their union to themselves, at least until she'd decided how to gently break it to her family and close friends.

Lillian smiled at Geraldine. "Perhaps we should find a more comfortable place to get to the bottom of whatever happened at The Orphan Ranch?"

"Of course, of course," Dina instantly responded. "Everyone can make themselves at home in the parlor while I put on water for coffee and tea. I believe there are still a few of the biscuits Cook brought over the other day. They are truly a gift from heaven."

"My new cousin and Cook is something else we need to talk about," Abby whispered into Lillian's ears.

"But your marriage first. And don't think you'll distract us," Lillian whispered back before stepping closer to Dina and putting an arm around the woman's shoulders. "Why don't we go into the kitchen? It's where we usually have our talks."

Dina wrung her hands and bit her lip as she glanced over at Abby. "The kitchen is rather small, and I'm afraid there aren't enough chairs for everyone. The parlor isn't much bigger, but we can all find a place to sit in there."

"Not to worry, Dina." Maggie smiled. "You mentioned that very problem the last time we dropped in, so I had Ian load some chairs into the wagon. They'll be fine for the short while you'll have them." She turned and winked at Abby. "He's makin' better ones for a weddin' present."

Abby threw her arms around the Irish woman in a big hug. "Thank you. It's so hard to find furnishings with so many people coming to San Francisco every day. It's a wonderful gift."

Beth clapped her hands together. "Then the kitchen it is. You get everything started, and I'll tell Little Jake to bring the chairs in from the wagon."

As Beth headed out the front door, the others took the short walk to the kitchen. Maggie and Dina went straight to the stove, while Abby urged Lillian and Rayne to sit at the table.

The newest bride smiled at Lillian. "Have you told Charles yet that he's going to be a papa?"

"I had to, thanks to you," Lillian laughed.

"Me?" Abby had no idea what she'd done to prompt that particular discussion.

"As soon as the supply wagons left, he dragged me into the parlor and demanded to know why I hadn't insisted Hercules be saddled so I could go check on you and George." Lillian shook her head. "I had no choice but to explain the reason to him."

"And what did he say?" Abby prompted.

"Nothing. My husband didn't make a sound because he was in a complete daze. He couldn't get out an understandable word for hours." Lillian joined the laughter that burst around the room. "And he's acted as if I'm made of glass ever since, just like I knew he would."

Rayne nodded and gently patted her own, slightly rounded belly. "Those brothers are cut out of the same log. Tremain is that way too. I had to threaten to saddle Sandbone and leave in the middle of the night if he didn't bring me to town the minute we heard about George." She grinned at Abby's frown. "Charles sent us word. I had to compromise though, and agree to ride the whole trip in the wagon."

135

Dina walked over and set a hot cup of tea in front of Rayne. "It seems there's a lot of compromising going on lately. Over trips to town, over weddings, and who knows what else."

Five pairs of eyes turned to Abby, and chairs were pulled into a tighter circle around the kitchen table.

Realizing there was no distracting them from learning the whole story behind her marriage to Cade, Abby silently searched for a way to put it in the best light.

"He rode out to the ranch just to be sure I got there safely," she said, then congratulated herself on her approach when smiles popped up across the circle. But her success was short-lived when Dina let out a loud snort.

"Nothing romantic about how that dense US Marshal cousin of mine asked her to marry him. Why, he didn't even ask her at all."

Abby groaned while demands for an explanation exploded around her.

Dina held up a hand and waited until the din faded away. "He made a bargain with Abby."

"Bargain?" Beth frowned. "What kind of bargain?"

"A trade of services, I'd guess you'd call it," Dina said.

"What?" Lillian jumped up from her seat and leaned across the table, her gaze fixed on Abby. "Exactly what services did he want you to exchange?"

"It's not as terrible as you think. I know how much all of you worry when I travel to visit my patients, so Cade offered his name and protection. This way I can see my patients whenever I need to, and no one will sprout gray hair over it," Abby said, recalling George's comment on the matter. "And Cade needed a doctor to be close by for Jules. It's a sound bargain."

Beth pursed her lips and narrowed her eyes. "Maybe you should have asked me to draw up formal papers for this bargain. Then you wouldn't have needed to sacrifice yourself to a marriage of convenience."

"It isn't a sacrifice," Abby protested with a scowl.

"Well, that's good to hear," Maggie said, looking around the group. "So our Doctor Abby *does* have feelin's for the man, I'm thinkin'."

Lillian slowly sat back down. "Abby. It doesn't make any difference whether or not a husband provides protection for you. We'll still worry every time you go out in the middle of the night, or travel across the hills, no matter what the reason. Nothing you do will make us change how we love you. And you know that."

Abby sighed and nodded. Of course she knew that. The same way she would always worry about each of them. It came with being part of a family.

"You're smart, caring and beautiful in every way. You also were very happy living in your cottage and taking care of us, and your other patients," Lillian pointed out. "So why did you marry Cade McKenzie?"

"I don't know." Abby hated to admit such a thing, especially out loud, but it was the truth. She really didn't know why she'd talked herself into accepting Cade's bargain.

"Nothin' in those books of yours to explain such behavior, then?" Maggie grinned.

"Well, you may not know why you married Cade, but I can tell you one thing for certain from my experience with the man. He doesn't do anything unless he wants to, so he wanted to marry you," Dina stated. "And he needs to give you a proper proposal."

"We'll all certainly agree on that," Beth said, reaching over and giving Abby's hand a firm squeeze.

"I haven't met the marshal yet. Is he goin' to be difficult to get a real proposal out of?" Maggie asked.

Grateful for the change of topic, no matter how temporary she thought it would be, Abby smiled at her friends. "I'm not sure. But Carrie said there's signs."

All five women leaned in closer.

"Do tell," Lillian said. "We need to hear every one of them."

Chapter Seventeen

Late into the afternoon, Cade strode up the walkway leading to the house where he'd first encountered his soon-to-be wife. He'd already been home, and wasn't surprised when he'd found it empty and a note from Abagail stating his brother and cousin were visiting Cook's household, and she was seeing patients that afternoon. He hoped his wife was practicing some sense of caution, and wasn't traveling about the city alone to check on her patients.

He walked into the open room. There was one man occupying a chair, who quickly ducked his head, lowering his hat brim down over his face. Cade's eyes narrowed but his gaze changed direction when his wife came through the door to the back hallway. Her attention has fixed on a book in her hands. Cade barely had time to smile at the picture she made before a well-dressed man walked out right behind her.

Taking two steps closer, Cade stopped and crossed his arms over his chest as he looked the stranger over. The man was around his own age, dressed in a tailored coat and pants, a sharply pressed shirt with gold cuff links, and black boots shined to a high gloss. He seemed just the sort who would appeal to a female doctor from back East. He was also standing far too close to Abagail, who was completely focused on her book and didn't seem to notice.

But Cade did.

"I can't thank you enough for allowing me to borrow your father's book, Mr. Renton," Abby said.

"Believe me, it's my pleasure, Dr. Metler. I hope you'll call on me any time." He paused until she looked up at him. "If you need any more of his books, of course. And what can I do to persuade you to call me Tom?"

"Nothing." Cade's tone was as hard and flat as his stare.

Abby blinked behind her spectacles, then smiled at Cade. A smile she hadn't given to Tom Renton. It soothed his simmering temper enough he didn't cross the space dividing them and put himself between the man and Abagail. It also helped when she took several steps away from her admirer.

"Cade. I was hoping you'd come by." Abby gestured to the man standing next to her. "This is Thomas Renton. I asked him for one of his father's books. Dr. Renton was an excellent physician before he passed away a few months ago. Mr. Renton, this is Cade McKenzie. He's a US Marshal."

"And her husband," Cade said with a pointed look at the frozen Tom Renton.

"Your husband?" The question came out with a squeak at the end.

"Well, yes, he is," Abby said.

Tom Renton immediately stepped back. "I had no idea you were married, Dr. Metler… that is, um, Mrs. McKenzie."

He fumbled his way past Abby, careful to keep a proper distance between them, and then made a wide path around Cade.

"Congratulations. To both of you, of course. Couldn't be happier to hear such wonderful news." Tom nodded and kept nodding all the way out the door.

Cade turned to Abby, surprised to see her frown.

"I was about to tell him we're married. There wasn't any need to frighten him."

"How did I do that?" Cade asked. "I only said three words to the man."

Abby put her hands on her hips. "And looked at him like you were going to shoot him."

"I wasn't going to shoot him just for bringing you a book, Abagail," Cade said, although to himself he thought it wasn't a bad idea at all. There must be a law somewhere about a man standing too close and making eyes at another man's wife.

"What happened to the patient who was waiting?" Abby looked past Cade to the empty chairs.

Cade cast a glance in that direction then shrugged. "Someone was here when I walked in. He must have left while I was explaining to Renton that you're married. Maybe he got discouraged by the news, too." But there was something about that man that nagged at the edges of Cade's memory.

"Where's Dr. Melton?" Cade asked.

"He wanted to get out for a while. I believe he went to see a friend."

Cade looked around. "So you've been here by yourself all afternoon?"

Abby sighed and shook her head at him. "Cade, I've been here by myself, seeing patients, many times. And if you weren't standing here, I'd lock up by myself, which I've also done many times. Now I'm hoping my husband will accompany me to my cottage so I can pick up a few things."

He nodded, walking over to the window while she gathered up her medical bag and the book Renton had brought her. He glanced at the chair vacated by the man who'd left. Could be he wasn't too keen on talking with a lady doctor when he'd found out her husband was around. But there was something about him…

"Are you ready? We shouldn't be too late. I don't want Dina to worry," Abby said.

Once outside they walked along together, with Cade leading his horse. After a slight tug-of-war, he managed to wrest the medical bag from his wife and tie it onto the back of his saddle. But only after promising her he would have it in her hands at the speed of lightning if she needed it.

After a few minutes of silently struggling with himself, he opened his mouth and then closed it again.

"You can say whatever it is that's on your mind, Cade," Abby said, keeping her own gaze straight ahead.

"Is your cottage far from here?" Cade asked.

Abby shook her head. "It's only a quarter hour walk."

"Did you like living there?" He touched the scar on his face as he considered what he really wanted to say to her.

"I did. Cade, what is it?" Abby stopped and faced him.

"It's not so easy buying a bed."

"What?" her forehead wrinkled as she peered into his face.

Cade looked away and then back at her. "I never thought much about having a wife. It's not an easy thing."

Abby's eyes narrowed and her hands were back on her hips. "What is it that you find so difficult, Marshal?"

She looked so put out with him that Cade couldn't stop the grin. "Walking to your place, for one thing."

His wife rolled her eyes and started moving again. "You're free to mount your horse if you want to."

He laughed and captured one of her hands. "What I mean, Abagail, is that I never gave any thought on how you actually got around to see your patients. Whether you walked, rode or took a buggy."

"Oh." Abby smiled up at him. "Well, I live close to Lillian and Charles. I keep Marron in their stable, and Danny can hitch a carriage horse any time I need one."

"Or that we'd need a bed. It's going to take a month or so to get one. They're in short supply," Cade said. "Not much luck either on finding another chair for the table."

"Don't worry about it, Cade. Maggie brought some over," Abby said. "Here we are."

She stopped in front of a nice sized cottage, with a large window in front and a neat picket fence enclosing a small garden. He followed her, carrying her medical bag and smiling at the scraggly row of flowers lining the walkway, their buds drooping over on either side. He guessed growing things wasn't one of his wife's many talents.

Once Cade stepped inside, he stopped to take in the cozy atmosphere. He silently approved of the simple rocker with the table and lamp, and the shelves filled with books. Beyond it was a compact kitchen and another sitting area, boasting a small divan and two straight-backed chairs with needlepoint covers on the seats. Abby directed him to set the bag by the front door and kept on walking to the back of the room. He did as he was told then followed her, curious to see the rest of her house. When he passed through the doorway on the other side of the kitchen, he stopped and looked at her.

"Abagail."

Abby turned. "Yes, Cade?"

"You have a bed."

Abby glanced over at the bed. Suddenly it seemed to take up every inch of space in the room. Not sure what to say, or where to look, she settled for taking several deep breaths. She felt calmer until she heard the decided *thunk* of a heavy boot being dropped. Abby whirled around, her hand going to her stomach when Cade's second boot hit the floor.

"What are you doing?" She quickly leaned over and picked up one boot, holding it out to him, gaping when he ignored her and peeled off his socks. "You can't walk to Lillian's in your bare feet."

Cade stood and unbuttoned his shirt as he walked to the door. He discarded his shirt, draping it over the doorknob before his hands went to his gun belt.

Since he was blocking the door, Abby had no way to gracefully exit the room as her husband continued to discard pieces of clothing. Her eyes slammed shut when he dropped his britches. The sound of him stepping out of them had her breathing spike so hard she was afraid she might be in danger of fainting.

"How long are you going to keep your eyes closed? I thought you'd seen everything in those medical books."

It was the humor in his voice that had Abby's eyes snapping open.

"I'm a doctor. I've certainly seen..." She stammered into silence as she took in the full view of broad shoulders, and the ripple of muscles down his torso.

After several long moments, Cade grinned. "Through comparing me to those pictures in your books?"

"I'm doing no such thing. It's just that you, I mean you're so..."

Again she found herself trailing off, unable to speak as she stared at him in wonder. She'd seen a fully naked man once before. But he wasn't like Cade. Everywhere her eyes touched were starkly defined ridges of muscle. He was pure strength come to life. Acutely aware of his raw, male presence, Abby's breathing went to short quick bursts as she stood, rooted to the spot, hugging his boot.

Cade slowly walked forward, holding her gaze with his. When he was so close his bare chest touched the hand she'd wrapped around his boot, he ran a single finger softly down her cheek.

"I've wanted you from the moment I saw you."

"I, I..." Abby felt the heat continue to build as it streamed outward through her limbs. "Cade, I don't know..."

"Shh." He took her glasses off and bent slightly backwards to place them safely on the bureau. He started to take the pins out of her hair.

"Even when I thought you were married to someone else, I wanted you."

"Cade." She gasped when his lips touched a spot behind her ear.

Her hair fell in a soft whisper down her back. He ran a hand over the silky mass then slipped under it and slowly traced the graceful curve of her spine, finally lifting his hands free and cupping them around her face, his fingers light and warm against her cheeks.

"Lord, you're beautiful."

Cade bent and kissed her, claiming her mouth, exploring every inch of it with his tongue. He kept kissing her, never letting up as he set his boot aside and removed her blouse. She made a weak protest when her skirt dropped to the floor, but forgot it as the kisses deepened.

And she didn't want him to stop. She wrapped her arms around his neck and pulled him closer. He locked his arms around her back, and now she did gasp out loud as her bare breasts pressed tight against his chest.

He bent his knees and picked her up, his mouth locked to hers as he laid her on the bed and carefully positioned his body on top of her.

She was still for a moment, absorbing the feel of his weight. It was wonderful. Abby gave in to the new sensations and ran her hands along the hard muscles of his back. Cade groaned softly and began to kiss a path down her body.

By the time he made his way back up to her mouth, Abby was on fire, gasping so loudly for breath she was positive she'd never get enough air again.

"Cade, please." Abby squirmed beneath him, not even sure what it was she was asking.

"Look at me, Abagail."

When she raised glazed eyes to his, he caged her with his arms and leaned down to whisper in her ear.

"You're mine."

When he lifted his head and looked into her eyes, she lifted a hand and traced a finger across his scar. "Yes, Cade. I am."

He took her mouth again with his, and with a single quick thrust, proceeded to make love to his wife.

***

Abby woke with a start, but when she tried to move she realized she was being held firmly in place. Confused, she reached up to untangle herself and encountered the warmth of bare skin. Her eyes flew open. Her first sight was a heavily muscled arm. Suddenly realizing she was naked as the day she was born, and lying in bed with Cade, Abby felt a trickle of warmth sneak its way across her cheeks.

"Something the matter?" Cade's lazy voice was close to her ear.

"No. I was just… that is I'm…" Much to her annoyance and frustration, Abby found herself speechless again.

Cade chuckled and removed his arm, stretching it overhead as Abby gathered the quilt more firmly around her and rolled over to face him.

"What I was trying to say is that I'm not used to sleeping with a man." Abby sniffed, proud she'd managed to complete an entire sentence.

He shrugged before pulling her against his side and anchoring an arm around her shoulders. "We're married."

Abby rolled her eyes in the dark. "A few words said by the preacher does nothing to make me used to sleeping with a man, Cade."

"True, sweetheart. But then I'm your husband, so you'll have to get used to sleeping with me." Over her head, Cade yawned.

"I suppose you're used to sleeping with a woman," Abby groused.

When he remained silent, she poked him in the chest. "Well?"

"You aren't expecting me to answer that, are you?"

She tilted her head back and looked up at him. "It's a simple enough question."

Cade laughed. "And one that's gotten many men in hot water ever since Adam and Eve."

Mentally conceding he was probably right, and she didn't really want to know anyway, Abby snuggled next to him again. "I guess we'd better get up soon."

"Why? It's not even dawn yet," Cade said.

Abby raised up on one elbow and leaned closer to peer into his face. "We can't leave Jules and Dina alone all night."

"We can if there's guards around the house."

"Are there guards around the house?" she asked, not sure he was being serious, but then not really surprised when he nodded.

146

"I arranged for them yesterday. They're going to be there whenever I'm not," Cade said.

For Dina and Jules's sake, Abby thought it was an excellent idea. Still, they needed to get back to the house. "They'll be expecting us. We'll have to come up with an excuse for missing dinner with them as it is."

Cade tightened his arm and drew her closer for a thorough kiss. "No, we won't. I borrowed your habit and left a note telling Dina we'd be late and not to wait up." He pressed her head back onto his shoulder. "Now try to get more sleep. You don't want to be too exhausted to see your patients."

Laughing, Abby relaxed, enjoying his warmth as she closed her eyes.

***

"Cade, wake up. We need to go."

Abby stood by the side of the bed and watched her husband open one eye and then the other.

"I made breakfast, if that will help."

"Breakfast?" Cade sniffed the air then looked over at his wife. "Is that coffee?"

"And biscuits. I also have a jar of jam to go with them." Nodding, Abby went back to the kitchen, not wanting the biscuits to burn. She wasn't entirely sure how to make them but knew they were basically flour, water and a little salt. At least she thought that's what Cook had told her once. Since they looked right, she must have remembered most of it.

Cade strolled in a few minutes later, buckling his belt. He looked out the front window and frowned. "It's later than I thought."

"You sleep very soundly," Abby said, pouring a thick brown liquid into a mug.

"I usually sleep pretty light," Cade said, still frowning at the sunshine spilling in through the window. He took the mug Abby handed him and absently raised it to his lips.

Abby turned to put the biscuits onto a plate so missed the silent grimace from her husband, along with his hard stare into the coffee mug.

Cade picked up a biscuit and weighed it in his hand. When he dropped it back onto the plate, it made a very loud thud. He doubted if his horse would eat one.

"We can take the biscuits with us. We should check on Jules and Dina." Cade walked over and set his mug into the kitchen sink.

"Just a minute, Abagail."

Seeing the serious look on his face, Abby stood a little straighter, sure she was about to get another lecture on having an escort every time she set foot out of the house. After the pure magic of last night, she didn't want to have a fight this morning.

Her husband moved to stand in front of her and reached into his shirt pocket. Her hand flew to her throat, and her eyes locked with his, when he pulled out a solid gold band. Lifting her left hand, he slipped it onto her finger then leaned down for a soft, lingering kiss.

"Another ritual I remembered."

Abby lifted her hand and admired the ring before smiling up at him. "It's beautiful, Cade. Thank you."

"My pleasure, Mrs. McKenzie."

Happy beyond any words she could find, Abby took his hand in hers.

"Shall we go?"

Together they walked to the Jamison's stables to hitch up the carriage and take Marron to his new home.

Chapter Eighteen

Abby leaned against her husband's side, enjoying the quiet ride through the last, drifting tendrils of the morning fog. They'd just pulled up in front of the house when she felt Cade's arm suddenly tense. She looked up at him, then followed the line of his gaze to a lone horse and rider at the far end of the street. Abby squinted behind the glass of her spectacles, but the man was too far away to make out his features. All she could clearly see were the very distinctive markings on his horse, with the front and back of its body in two different shades of grey.

"Do you know that man?" Abby asked.

"He's not your worry."

As Cade maneuvered the carriage toward the small stable at the back of the house, the stranger lifted a hand to the brim of his hat, along with a brief nod, before urging his horse around and disappearing down the street. Abby wondered at the taut line of Cade's jaw, but he remained silent. Even as he unhitched the high-stepping Daisy and led her into a stall next to Marron's, her husband didn't say a word.

Deciding he'd slipped on his Marshal McKenzie face and had no intention of confiding in her, Abby did a mental sigh. Picking up her medical bag from the floor of the carriage, she made her way to the house, leaving him to deal with the rest of her books and clothes. Her mood turned brighter at the sight of Dina and Jules sitting at the kitchen table.

"Good morning." Abby smiled as she set her bag down near the door. "How was your night?"

Dina raised an eyebrow. "Fine. Just fine, wasn't it Jules?"

The boy bobbed his head. "And I'm eating my broth and meat. But I sure would like a piece of bread. Can I have one? Dina said I had to ask you."

Before Abby could answer, Cade came through the door carrying a large satchel under one arm and a stack of books under the other.

"Where have you been, Cade?" Jules demanded.

"Jules, why don't you get your school books together. Cook said he'd be here early to take you over to study with Ammie's tutor this morning," Dina said.

When his lip stuck out in a distinct pout, Abby reached over and patted his hand. "Go on, Jules. It will give us a chance to decide on that piece of bread you want."

Once again wreathed in smiles, Jules slid off his chair. "I'm all better. Ammie and Cook said I can even take lessons from Master Kwan, if you say it's all right, Cade."

His older brother set the books on the table and Abby's satchel on the floor. "We'll see."

Clapping his hands together, Jules raced out the door and down the hallway.

"Yes, Cade, where have you been?" Dina asked. "I expected you both last night."

"We had to get Abby's things." Cade picked up the satchel and looked at Abby. "I'll put this in Dina's room, until we get everything we need for a proper bedroom. Then I have a business matter to attend to."

With a brief nod to both women, Cade strode after his younger brother, while Dina stared at his retreating back with her mouth half-open.

Lifting the coffee pot sitting in the middle of the table, Dina poured a cup and pushed it toward Abby. "Well?"

Suddenly cold, Abby gratefully wrapped her hand's around the steaming mug, taking a sip before answering Dina's unspoken question. "We stopped by my cottage and decided to spend the night there."

Dina frowned. "Why? I've never known Cade to stay away when he could be home with Jules."

Abby cleared her throat and clutched her mug a bit tighter. "There was a bed."

"Well we have beds here... Oh. I see."

Much to Abby's surprise, Dina looked more amused than embarrassed. They both glanced down the hallway at the sound of boots rapidly descending the stairs. Abby stood up and hurried toward the front of the house, catching Cade as he stepped into the foyer. She managed to latch onto his arm before he went out the door.

"Cade, where are you going?"

"There's some things I need to see to," Cade said. "I want you to stay inside today."

Abby shook her head. "I have patients to see."

Cade put both his hands on her shoulders and locked his eyes with hers. "I'll stop by and let Dr. Melton know you'll be staying home today."

"But Cade, I can't just stop seeing my patients whenever..." Her words were cut off when he bent and pressed a hard, quick kiss on her mouth.

"We'll talk later. Right now I have to go, Abagail."

"If you happen to run into Beth or John, be sure to thank them for the nice bed." Dina called out.

When Cade frowned at her, Dina smiled back at him. "They had it sent over yesterday, as a wedding gift."

With a ghost of a smile Cade shut the door behind him, leaving both women to stare at the empty space where he'd been standing.

Abby couldn't believe what she'd heard. The man could not be serious. Didn't he listen to her at all? Dina put a comforting arm around her shoulders.

"Let's finish our coffee."

A few moments later they were sitting at the kitchen table. Abby absently sipped at her coffee while she thought over Cade's strange mood swings. Earlier that morning he'd been smiling and, well, romantic, when he had given her the ring. Now barely an hour had passed and he was snapping and closed off. Not like the man she'd made love with the night before. But then he'd acted much the same at the ranch—angry one moment, and asking her to marry him in the next.

"First time I've ever known my cousin to leave the house before he had coffee," Dina remarked. "But then he's having a lot of 'firsts' lately.

Abby adjusted her glasses as she peered at the older woman. "What do you mean? I haven't noticed anything different about him."

"That's because you didn't know him before he met you," Dina laughed.

She set her coffee cup down and started counting off on her fingers. "Since he's been home from the army, he's always had an even temper. Now he's as changeable and skittish as a stray cat. Never known him to have a jealous bone in his body, but from what you said, he took an instant dislike to Luke because he helped you down from the supply wagon. And he's never spent a night away from Jules, if he could help it."

"You think I've completely disrupted his life?" Abby asked. The very idea had her spirits sinking.

"And he's disrupted yours right back. But the two of you will find a way to manage together." Dina smiled. "Since you're staying home today, it might be the perfect time to give Jules a new food. What's your opinion of bread?"

Temporarily distracted, Abby's thoughts turned to her young brother-in-law and patient.

***

It was still early in the afternoon when Cade stepped out of the bright sunlight and into the subdued lighting of *The Crimson Rose*. Even at this hour, eager players crowded around roulette wheels and squinted at cards dealt to them at the various tables hosting the popular game of faro.

Looking around, Cade decided there were different kinds of gold mines from those in the mountains to the east. And Jamison owned one of them right here in town.

"Looking for a game, Marshal?"

Cade turned to find Charles Jamison standing behind him, his deep brown eyes watching closely.

"I came looking for you. Is there some place more private we can talk?" Cade asked.

Charles inclined his head and led the way through an archway near the entrance. He opened the first door on the right, and stepped inside the spacious room. A large desk dominated the center, along with a separate seating area. Charles headed there, settling himself into a cushion-backed chair as he indicated for Cade to sit in the one across from him.

The marshal took in the dark wood and generally masculine feel of the space, right down to the line of crystal decanters and carefully stacked glasses on the sideboard.

"You do well," Cade observed.

Charles smiled. "*We* do well, Marshal. My wife had already made her fortune when I met her. I needed to catch up."

"And my husband has made one of his own since he arrived in San Francisco." Lillian Jamison strolled into the room, softly closing the door behind her.

She walked over to her husband and gave him a kiss before perching on the chair's wide armrest. Her crystal blue eyes stared back at Cade. He silently studied her for a long moment, not surprised when Lillian didn't blush or turn away. She was definitely a woman used to being looked at.

"You wanted to talk?" Charles stated, his arm coming around Lillian's waist. "That is if you're through staring at my wife."

"I apologize," Cade said. "I was just noticing she has the same look as Abagail."

Lillian's slow smile had Cade ducking his head. Suddenly remembering he was still wearing his hat, he snatched it off his head then fumbled to catch it as it jumped out of his hands and fell to the ground.

Annoyed by his sudden clumsiness, he leaned over, picked up his hat and placed it on a table next to the chair. He also didn't take well to the big grin on Jamison's face. At Cade's glare, the gambler only shrugged.

"The women in this family always turn the men into bumbling fools at one time or another," Charles said. "Which reminds me. I haven't had a chance yet to welcome you into the family."

Cade sighed. "Thank you." Determined to change the subject, he narrowed his gaze on Charles. "Have you had any problems lately with Ben Linder and his men?"

The gambler shook his head. "Not that I've heard. John hasn't mentioned it either. I assumed they were still in the hills near the ranch."

"And now you don't think so?" Lillian asked.

"I'm sure I spotted Linder near my house this morning. And I saw another one of his men waiting for Doctor Abby yesterday."

Charles and Lillian exchanged a look.

"Since we haven't heard of more robberies, maybe he's here to find out if the rumors are true that there's a US Marshal in town," Charles speculated.

"But why was he at Abby's?" Lillian wondered. "It isn't common knowledge yet that the two of you are married, so why would he be following her? Maybe it was a coincidence?"

"What did he say about why he was there?" Charles asked.

The marshal pursed his lips into a thin line. "I didn't get a chance to ask him."

"Why not?" Lillian tilted her head to one side and raised an eyebrow.

"I was too busy explaining to Thomas Renton why he shouldn't be flirting with my wife," Cade stated. "And if it *was* a coincidence and Linder didn't know I had a wife, he does now."

"What are you doing about it?" Charles demanded. "I can arrange for more guards."

"I'd appreciate that. And I'd appreciate you talking to those eyes and ears you have all over town. Maybe they've seen him, or heard he was wandering the streets. For the time being, I told Abby to stay in the house today, and she'll be staying inside until I catch Linder."

Lillian let out a short laugh. "Abby will insist on going out to check on her patients."

Cade shook his head. "They'll have to come to her. And the guards will be told to make sure she stays inside."

Cade wasn't going to give way on this point. Abagail's safety was far too important. He'd had a cold feeling in his veins ever since he'd seen Linder, especially when it finally came to him why the man in Abagail's waiting room looked so familiar.

"You can't keep her a prisoner in the house, Marshal McKenzie," Lillian stated. "And if you try, she's going to regret ever agreeing to that bargain of yours and marrying you. She just might figure out a way to undo the whole thing, and I'll be happy to help her."

"My part of that bargain was to keep her safe. I can't do that if she's running all over town when Linder is free and so close," Cade said, ignoring the fact Lillian seemed to know all about his business, and keeping his voice low and calm. He glanced over at Charles who shook his head in response.

"That responsibility goes with being a husband," Lillian countered. "And so does spending time to get to know your wife so you won't make ridiculous demands she can't possibly keep. Even telling her about Linder's man showing up at her practice won't make Abby stop seeing her patients. Especially those who can't get around very well. She'll be more cautious if you ask her to be, *and* explain why, but it won't stop her. It's what makes Abby the person she is. And you can either love her the way she is, or let her find another man who will."

Lillian rose and gathered her full skirt up in one hand before sweeping out of the room, not bothering to close the door behind her.

"I can't say I blame you, Marshal. There was a time when I thought Lillian was in danger because of me, and I wanted to keep her locked up or chained to my side." Charles leaned back into his chair and studied the tall man across from him. "But the women have their own ideas about things, and you'll need to respect that if you want them to love you back."

Cade thought the gambler was a fool if he took that kind of risk with his wife's life. "And did you apologize and let her have her way?"

"I find a little groveling along with an apology also helps," Charles grinned.

"I don't grovel." Cade got to his feet. And he sure wasn't going to apologize for something he was right about.

Charles stood up as well. "It also might keep you from sleeping alone in a cold bed if you fit a proper proposal somewhere into your busy schedule."

Distracted by the change in subject, Cade frowned. "We're already married. Why would I propose?"

The gambler gave him what Cade interpreted as a pitying look. "The women in this family not only have their own ideas about how to live their lives, they are also very keen on proper proposals. Not one of them will give you any peace until Abby gets one."

Cade rolled his eyes heavenward in a bid for patience. Proposals in the middle of tracking killers? He knew what his priorities were, and they didn't run to romantic gestures.

Charles slapped a hand on the marshal's shoulder.

"Let's see what we can do about arranging for more guards," he said, walking with Cade back out into the gambling hall. They both stopped just inside the large double front doors. "I'll contact John this morning."

"I appreciate it." Cade put on his hat and stepped into the sunlight.

Chapter Nineteen

"Well?"

Hal shot the single word question at him before Ben even had a chance to dismount his horse. Ignoring him, Ben walked over to the ebbing campfire and squatted next to it. He jerked his head toward a tin pot that was charred, and with more than a few dents around its sides. It was resting slightly sideways in the embers, its lid rattling gently. Tommy stuck his lip out, but he still grabbed a cloth and lifted the pot to pour out a cup of the boiling brew. He handed it to Ben.

"I ain't no woman who's supposed to pour out coffee." Tommy's lip edged out even further. "You can git your own plate if you want some of them beans."

Ben shrugged and blew on the steaming cup, glancing over at Hal from beneath the brim of his hat.

"Where's Walt and Jed?"

"They're out scouting the road, Ben," Tommy answered. "Like you said to."

"They should be back soon." Hal walked over and stood a few feet away from the youngest man in the gang but kept his gaze directed at Ben. "Did you see him? I told you there was a US Marshall in town. And I saw him in that female doc's office you sent me to. He's that same marshal who killed Frank, ain't he?"

"It's him," Ben said, his voice hard. A couple of the men the marshal hired were a little too chatty with the storekeepers near the boarding house where he and Hal had stayed. It hadn't been hard to have a few coins exchange hands for information on McKenzie. It was just his good luck that the marshal had walked into that doctor's office right when Hal was sitting there, and then the lawman had been pulling up to his house with his wife just as Ben was about to hunker down and watch the place. He'd found out everything he needed to know right then.

McKenzie must have followed Ben to San Francisco and somehow gotten himself married. And now Ben knew where the marshal and that pretty little doctor wife of his lived.

"So are we goin' to be headin' north again? What about them mountains and that snow?" Tommy asked.

"We're gittin' low on places to run," Hal said. "And that's a fact."

Ben rose to his feet and looked off into the distance. Now was his chance to even the score for Frank, and he meant to take it.

"Wouldn't be needin' a place to run if it weren't for the marshal. If he's gone, they ain't likely to send another one soon." Ben nodded at the other two.

"How do we make him gone?" Hal asked. "He's always got a pack of men around him, and I ain't fixin' on bein' in another gunfight with him." Hal spat onto the ground and crossed his arms over his barrel of a chest.

"We kill that marshal and I'm thinkin' they'll send a whole bunch of them after us," Tommy whined. "We can't kill no US Marshal."

"They won't send anyone if they don't know what happened to him. And even if they do, they won't know it was us that got rid of him," Ben said.

Hal snorted. "How we gonna do that?"

"We rob a few miners."

Tommy looked from Ben to Hal, then started kicking dirt into the fire. "All right, let's git goin'. Don't see what this does about the marshal, though."

Ben reached over and pulled Tommy back from the fire. "Not you. There's somethin' else you need to do. You can meet up with us later."

Chapter Twenty

Abby looked up from the kitchen table when Cade pushed open the backdoor. The sun had set hours ago, and he brought the chill of the night in with him. She watched silently as he crossed the room and dropped into one of the chairs. He didn't say a word but lifted her hand and laced his fingers with hers. Something was troubling him. Abby could see it in his face.

Seemingly oblivious to the tension radiating from her cousin, Dina came bustling over, dropping a sack of flour and several small containers onto the table.

"This is everything," she declared.

"Are you sure?" Abby looked over the items lined up in front of her. With one hand she moved them around, placing them in groups, then frowning and rearranging them again.

"What are you doing?" Cade asked.

Both women ignored him as they bent closer to examine the basic cooking ingredients.

"Do you really believe one of these is the cause?" Dina whispered. "How are we going to know for sure?"

"Logic and deduction." Abby nodded once, then stepped back and eyed each ingredient.

Abby heard her husband's heavy sigh just before his free hand cupped her chin and turned her face toward him. "What are you doing?"

"Looking for whatever caused Jules's breathing attack," Abby said.

Cade's eyes widened. He looked over at Dina who nodded back at him. "Is my brother all right?"

He started to get up but Abby placed a hand on his shoulder and pressed him back into the chair.

"Jules is fine. It was a mild attack and subsided quickly," Abby said, her gaze returning to the items on the table.

Her husband glanced down and frowned. "You think something here is causing Jules's problem?"

Abby nodded, picking up one of the small jars. "What is this? Pumpkin seeds?"

"Yes." Dina pointed to another jar. "That's sesame seeds, and in the crock is honey."

"Ladies. If Jules is fine and this can wait until morning, I'd like to get some rest. I need an early start tomorrow." Cade rose and pulled Abby along with him.

Wondering what was going on, Abby threw Dina an apologetic look and let herself be dragged up the stairs. He stopped long enough to be sure Jules was sleeping peacefully before continuing down the hall to the master bedroom at the far end.

Once inside with the door soundly shut, Cade let go of Abby's hand and lit the two, tall candles on either side of the bureau.

Abby stared at her husband. "Cade, what's going on?"

"I received word today that Ben Linder and his men robbed a group of miners heading into town from their claims. He left a couple of them in bad shape." Cade dropped onto the bed and removed his boots.

"Oh." Abby's nerves did a small jump in her stomach. "And you intend to hunt for him?"

Cade looked at her and frowned. "It's what I do, Abagail."

Abby was silent, carefully weighing her need to confront him about his ordering her to stay inside without any explanation or reason, against not wanting to have a fight when he was leaving for such a dangerous task.

She walked over to where he sat on the bed and placed her hands on the sides of his face. "You'll be careful?"

"I always am. I could do with a good night's sleep, though. Which I can no longer get unless you're lying naked beside me." Despite the sag in his shoulders, Cade grinned. "You're blushing, Mrs. McKenzie."

161

"No, I'm not," Abby insisted despite the heat in her cheeks. "It must be a trick of the light."

She marched over to the bureau, opened a drawer and pulled out one of the long cotton nightgowns she'd put away after Cade had left that morning. With no privacy screen in the room, she simply kept her back to him and drew the nightgown over her head, wiggling out of her clothes beneath the shelter of its cotton folds. It was awkward, but she finally managed it. When she was finished, she turned around to find him already in bed with the covers pulled up to his waist. His chest and arms were bare, and Abby was sure the rest of him was, too. He was watching her, a smile on his face.

"That was very interesting, Abagail. Does a lot to fire up a man's imagination."

Not knowing what to say, Abby walked over to the bed and slipped under the quilt when Cade held it aside.

She rolled over to the far edge but he reached out an arm and pulled her until she was snug against his chest with her backside nestled into his groin.

"Relax, sweetheart. I know you're still sore from last night," Cade whispered into her ear. "We're only going to sleep."

Feeling a twinge of disappointment, Abby nodded.

"You're too tired, anyway," she said quietly over her shoulder.

He chuckled. "No man is ever that tired, sweetheart."

Cade anchored his arm firmly around her waist, and within a minute Abby heard his light snore. Settling in more comfortably against him, she dropped off to sleep, a smile on her face.

***

When Abby woke the following morning, it was the first time she'd found herself alone in a bed after spending the night with her husband. Thinking he may have already left without saying goodbye, she hastily shoved the quilt aside and dashed across the room to the wardrobe. Grabbing the nearest skirt and blouse, Abby quickly dressed and headed downstairs. She peeked into the parlor but it was empty, so she kept on going into the kitchen.

Cade was standing by the table, a mug of coffee in his hand.

"Oh, there you are, dear," Dina said, wiping her hands on her apron. "I was going to wake you. You and Cade need to have a talk."

Abby stopped and looked from one to the other. "We do?"

"Dina, now isn't the time," Cade began, but his cousin cut him off.

"It's the only time you'll have. You need to give all your orders to your wife." Dina pointed a finger at him "And if you think I'm going to do it for you, then you'd better think again, Cade McKenzie."

Her face flushed and eyes blazing, Dina scooped up her coffee mug and marched out of the kitchen.

Abby turned a wary gaze on her husband. "Orders?"

Cade ran a hand through his hair before pulling a chair out. "You may as well sit."

"If you'll sit too," Abby said, not willing to be constantly looking up at him for what she had a feeling was going to be a very uncomfortable conversation.

"I don't have much time this morning. I have men waiting on me," Cade said, but he did grab another chair, pulled it away from the table and sat.

At least that's something, Abby thought.

"Is this about you hunting for Ben Linder?" Abby asked when Cade fell silent.

He nodded. "I have two groups of men I'll be meeting with this morning."

"Two?" Abby folded her hands in front of her. "So you can search more quickly?"

"No. We know where the gang was last spotted. We'll spread out from there. The second group is coming here. To guard the house."

"Well I'm sure we'd both sleep better knowing Dina and Jules are safe. Is Dina upset about strange men being in the house?" Abby asked, relieved it wasn't anything more than that. She could certainly do her best to calm down his cousin.

Cade looked away for a moment. "They'll be under strict orders not to let anyone leave."

"Oh." Abby thought that over. Now she knew why Dina was so upset. She wouldn't be able to visit with Cook and her new friend, Charlotte, until Cade returned.

"I'll explain it to her as best I can, Cade, but it isn't going to be easy. Of course if she needs anything, I'll bring it home after I've seen my patients."

"Abagail, the order won't be just for Dina and Jules. It will be the same for you, too."

She froze. She couldn't have heard Cade expected her to stay in this house for days? Surely he realized that would mean abandoning her patients? Determined to keep calm and reason with him, she drew in a deep breath and then another. When her racing heart slowed somewhat, she adjusted her glasses and refolded her hands.

"And why do any of us have to stay in the house?"

"The man at the end of the road yesterday morning was Ben Linder."

Abby gasped. "It was?"

Cade nodded. "When I saw him, I remembered why the man waiting at your practice for you yesterday looked so familiar. I don't know his name, but the last time I saw him was over a barrel of a rifle as he was galloping away with what was left of Linder's gang." He paused and looked over at her. "He knows we're married and where my family lives. You need to stay inside this house until I catch him."

"I understand your concern, but I have patients to see, Cade. I stayed in yesterday until you had a chance to explain. Now that you have, I'll take one of the guards with me whenever I leave the house."

Cade shook his head. "No."

Abby squeezed her hands together so tightly her fingers began to turn white. "You aren't being reasonable, Cade. You said yourself the gang is outside of town, robbing miners."

A tic in his cheek became more prominent as Cade's jaw hardened. "You'll stay in the house, Abagail."

She slowly rose to her feet and placed her hands flat on the table, leaning into them as she stared him straight in the eye. "I will not."

Cade stood and towered over her. "I'll make sure the guards know you, Dina and Jules are to stay where you're safe."

"Don't do this to us, Cade," Abby said softly. "Don't make me choose between you and my responsibility as a doctor."

"There isn't a patient in this world worth risking your life for, Abagail. You'll stay in the house where I can be sure you're protected." Cade wrapped his hands around her upper arms and lifted her off the floor. He gave her a quick kiss before setting her back on her feet. "I'll be gone a few days, at least. Maybe a week or so. I'll send word when I can."

In the next moment he'd disappeared out the backdoor. Abby caught a brief glimpse of him through the kitchen window, striding to the stable.

She waited another full minute before turning on her heel and walking down the hallway and up the stairs. She headed straight to the master bedroom and was on her hands and knees, struggling to reach the satchel she'd stowed away under the bed after she'd unpacked, when Dina came running into the room.

"Well?"

Abby looked over at her. "You heard the marshal. We're to stay in the house until he says otherwise." Finally managing a firm grip on the elusive bag, she pulled it out and set it on top of the rumpled quilt.

"What are you doing?" Dina asked, her eyes bouncing between Abby and the bag lying on its side on the bed.

"I'm packing to move back to my cottage before those guards get here. I have to come and go when I'm needed, Dina. Whether he's a husband or a marshal, Cade can't tell me what to do." Abby jumped to her feet and marched over to the bureau and began pulling out clothes.

"Because you have patients?" Dina asked. When Abby nodded, she put her hands on her hips and glared at the younger woman. "What about your patient here? What about Jules?"

Abby paused from making a tangled mess of her clothes and took a deep breath. She dropped the bunched-up nightgown onto the bureau and walked over to give Dina a hug. "Send word to me if he has another episode. I'll be here before you know it."

Dina returned the hug then held her at arm's length. "Why don't you just stay here and come and go as you please, despite what Cade says?"

Abby stuck her chin out. "You heard the marshal. He's going to have guards all around this place, with strict orders to keep us inside."

"And so?" Dina asked. "What will they do besides tell you to stay inside? Pull a gun on you? Believe me, they will never, never do that. Cade would beat them within an inch of their life if they did such a thing."

Abby's forehead crinkled in thought. "They could follow Cade's example and pick me up and make me stay in the house. It wouldn't surprise me if he'd told them that very thing."

"Not if I pull *my* gun on *them*," Dina said, then smiled when Abby gaped at her. "Of course I have a gun, and I know how to use it. After all, I do oversee the household of a US Marshal."

"Now you just consider that for a while," Dina went on. "I think those guards will be happy to accompany you to see your patients rather than put a hand on you, and then have to answer to your husband. Or get shot by me, of course."

"Of course," Abby grinned. It was an absolutely brilliant plan. And so simple. She would just tell the guard "no", and if he put up a fuss, Dina would hold him at bay while she made her escape. And if that didn't work, she'd send a note to her friends to come rescue her. That would be perfect. And she said as much to her cousin-in-law.

Dina clapped her hands. "Wonderful. Now, should we get back to examining our evidence on the kitchen table?"

Abby nodded. Dina's solution was a simple one. She wished crossing the widening gap between herself and her husband was as easy.

Chapter Twenty-One

With her eyes still closed, Abby stretched her arms over her head, arching her back off the bed. She opened one eye and looked across the vacant space beside her and sighed. She'd retired late, then lain awake for much of the night, finally falling to sleep as the dark sky outside the window lessened into tones of gray.

After Cade left, she'd spent the rest of the day and a good part of the evening, at the kitchen table. Not because her husband had ordered her to stay in the house, but to go over the ingredients Dina regularly used to make bread. After Jules's attack, with only the one, small change in his diet, Abby was sure the answer to his affliction was in that bread.

With her medical volumes stacked in front of her, she'd pored over reports of patients who suffered after eating particular foods or spices, searching for any mention of one of the ingredients lined up on the table. She'd read for hours until her back had felt as if it might break in two, and her eyes were tearing up behind her glasses. The long hours came to fruition when a lone case, in the book she'd borrowed from Thomas Renton, had given her what she was looking for. Abby had re-read the passage a dozen times, picking up the small jar of sesame seeds, setting it down, and then going over the reported symptoms again. Finally satisfied, she'd immediately sent a note off to Cook. He was the only person she knew who'd been around the world, including several voyages to the Far East. She was hoping he could confirm her suspicions.

Since she was sure the former seaman would send a response this morning, Abby pushed the quilt aside and walked over to the wash bowl.

"No reason to lie around, Abagail," she murmured to herself, smiling at her use of the formal version of her name that Cade favored.

But her smile didn't last long. The room was too empty without Cade in it. So early or not, she decided to get a start on her day. At least she could find something to occupy her thoughts other than her stubborn, thick-headed husband. Who was out, who knew where, looking for a man who wouldn't hesitate to shoot him. How could she ever get used to him being away and maybe never returning? And if she couldn't, what did that mean for their future? She had no intentions of sitting at home rather than seeing her patients, spending all of her days and nights worrying over him.

With no answer coming to her, she picked up the pitcher and poured a stream of water into the bowl. Even without her worries over the danger he'd put himself into, she didn't know if they'd be able to live together if he kept insisting she stayed wherever he wanted her to. Determined to push their dilemma out of her mind, she resolutely picked up the washcloth and scrubbed her face to a glowing pink.

Half an hour later she made her way to the kitchen, surprised to see Dina already sitting at the table, stirring her usual heaping tablespoon of sugar into her coffee.

"Good morning." Dina smiled. "There's plenty of coffee ready."

Crossing to the stove, Abby poured herself a full mug and carried it back to the table. She sat and took a moment to study Geraldine. She didn't like the slight pallor and pronounced circles under her new cousin's eyes.

"Are you feeling all right?"

"Just tired. I never sleep well when Cade is off chasing a group of dangerous men," Dina said.

Abby sighed and nodded.

"I usually bake when I need to keep my mind busy. Thought I'd get an early start on some biscuits. Cook gave me his recipe." Dina patted the pocket in her apron

169

"He did?" Abby's eyebrows shot up. She'd never known the man to write down any of his recipes, much less give them to someone else. But before she could question Geraldine any further, there was a sharp knock on the door leading to the back garden.

The two women exchanged a glance.

"Probably one of the guards," Dina said, rising to her feet.

Abby nodded, but frowned. It was too early for anyone to expect the residents of the household to be up and about.

Dina opened the door and said a very curt, "Can I help you?" as Abby strained to peek around her.

"I come for Dr. McKenzie. The marshal's wife?"

Hearing her name, Abby stood up, even as Dina crossed her arms and shook her head.

"Why do you need to see the doctor at this hour of the morning?" Dina asked. "Are you sick?"

Stepping up beside her cousin, Abby gently nudged her aside. "I'm the doctor."

The young man, with his hat still on his head and a gun belt sagging around his waist, was her height and stick thin. He was also in dire need of a bath.

"You married to the marshal?" he asked, his gaze dropping to her left hand.

Abby politely held it up, showing the wide gold band. "I am. And what's your name?"

Belatedly he took his hat off and gave a quick duck of his head. "Tommy. I'm Tommy."

"Well, Tommy. Do you need a doctor?" Abby asked.

"No. But your husband does. He was shot just as we was fixin' to come back into town."

Behind her Dina gasped as Abby's hands clenched into fists. "Shot? Cade's been shot? Where is he?"

Tommy bobbed his head up and down. "Yes ma'am. He was. About halfway to that ranch with all the kids on it. We got ambushed and had to run for it."

170

"Is he still alive?" Abby demanded, ignoring the sob behind her. She wouldn't believe Cade was dead. Even if the words were said, she still wouldn't believe it.

"He's alive. But he needs help if he's gonna stay that way. You need to come with me." He reached out but his hand only grabbed thin air since Abby had turned away to give Dina a hug.

"He's alive," Abby whispered, her eyes closed. "Cade's still alive."

She stepped back, but held onto Dina's shoulders. Abby took several large breaths in a futile attempt to calm her racing heart. Think. She had to think.

Whirling back around she faced Tommy. "I have to change and get my medical bag. Please saddle my horse. He's the big dark chestnut in the last stall. And be quick. I won't be long."

Abby lifted her skirt up to her knees and ran for the front foyer, leaving Dina behind as she took the stairs two at a time.

Dina's chin trembled, and tears trickled down her cheeks, as she watched Tommy walk back toward the stables. But there was something about the sight of him walking away that bothered her.

Slowly closing the door, she went over to the kitchen table and sat, resting her elbows on its top and covering her face with her hands. The fear, always present in the back of her mind ever since Cade took the oath of a US Marshal, dominated her thoughts. Cade had to be all right. She couldn't keep going if he never came home again. How would she and Jules manage?

Shaking with the cold sensation of fear, Dina reached for her coffee mug, sipping without thought and staring at the closed door to the back garden. Within minutes she heard the clatter of boots echoing down the hallway. Abby appeared, dressed in her boy's garb, carrying her tapestry bag in one hand and a rifle in the other.

Dina looked at her and blurted out what was on her mind. "I don't like this."

"I don't like Cade being hurt either, Dina. But I'll help him. We won't lose him. I promise." Abby's fierce expression reflected her inner resolve. She would keep that promise, no matter what it took.

"I know you will. But I don't like this Tommy. He gives me a bad feeling," Dina said slowly.

"You're just scared. So am I," Abby confessed. "But it's going to be fine. I'll bring Cade home."

Before Dina could grab hold of what was bothering her and put it into words, Abby had given her a quick, hard hug and was gone.

Another fifteen minutes went by before Dina got up from her chair and went to look out the kitchen window. Not seeing anyone, she made her way to the front parlor and peeked out those windows.

The front porch and street were deserted, but Dina wasn't looking for a passerby, she was looking for one of the guards. She waited by the window several more minutes before heading for the front door. Stepping out onto the porch, she walked from one end to the other, stretching over the rail to look around the side of the house. But she still didn't see anyone.

She went back inside and sat in the parlor, her gaze glued to the window. Another agonizingly slow ten minutes ticked by. A sudden movement by the front of the parlor had her choking back a startled cry of alarm when Jules appeared in the doorway.

"Dina? I'm hungry."

Goaded into action, she leaped to her feet and scurried over to the young boy, embracing him in a smothering hug. "Of course, of course. I'll get you something to eat."

"Dina. I can't breathe. Quit hugging me." Jules's voice was muffled against her apron.

Stepping back, Dina kept one arm around his shoulders as she propelled him toward the kitchen.

While Jules took a seat, she got out a pot to heat up the broth Cook had prepared. Thinking of the man made an idea take hold.

There was something not right about that Tommy person. He didn't look like someone Cade would hire. Not that she knew a great deal about men like that. But still, he just didn't seem right. And the way he'd walked off, as if he hadn't been in a hurry at all. Yes, she had a very bad feeling about Abby going along with that Tommy person. A very, very bad feeling. And tangled up with it was her fear for Cade. She couldn't sort it out. But she knew Cook could.

As she stirred the broth, Dina glanced over at Jules waiting patiently at the table, a spoon already in his hand. "Jules, did Cade ever show you how to hitch up a horse and buggy?"

"Yes ma'am," Jules grinned. "I can do it."

"That's good. Do you think you could help me hitch up Daisy?"

Her hand flew to her throat at a distinct knock on the front door. When Jules gave her a wide-eyed look, she instantly dropped her hand and pasted on a sunny smile. "I'll be right back. You go on and ladle out some of this broth and start eating your breakfast."

Dina wiped her hands on her apron as she slowly approached the front door. Opening it just a crack, she peered through the narrow slit then let out a sigh of relief when she recognized the man on the other side.

***

Standing on the porch of the marshal's house, Luke didn't mind running the small errand for Cook. Since it was on the way to *The Crimson Rose,* this extra stop wouldn't delay the start of his work by more than a few minutes. Having been raised on a farm, Luke was used to getting up early. He just hoped someone in the household was awake at this hour. But if not, he'd slip the note Cook had given him under the door and be on his way.

Luke wasn't prepared for the front door to be thrown open and Miss Geraldine come bursting through, throwing her arms around him and almost knocking him on his backside. Taking a quick step back to brace himself and keep on his feet, Luke was stunned for a moment before he gently peeled the woman away and held her at arm's length.

"Miss Geraldine? Are you all right?" Since Luke was currently staying in the house Cook ran for Charles Jamison's sister and niece, he'd met Geraldine when she'd brought Jules by for a visit. And she hadn't seemed like she was a bit touched in the head.

"Abby's gone with that man, and I think something's not right. She shouldn't have gone with him."

"Wait. Slow down." Luke held up a hand. "What man did Abby go with?"

Dina stepped away and wrung her hands. "The man Cade sent. Tommy. He said his name was Tommy."

Luke frowned. "The marshal sent a man here, and Abby went with him?"

"That's right. He said Cade was shot and needed a doctor, so Abby had to go with him. But I don't think she should have. He wasn't right. And he called her Dr. McKenzie. No one calls her that. And he walked to the stables when he should have been running. But the guards let them go, so maybe it was all right. But I don't think so." Dina looked up at him, her eyes round and her face pale.

"I was going to have Jules hitch up the wagon and go tell Cook. Something isn't right," she repeated.

Luke's brow furrowed into deep lines as he tried to make sense of her disjointed story.

"You're saying some man named Tommy came to the door and claimed Cade had sent him, and the marshal was shot?" If that's what the man said, Luke didn't doubt for a

174

minute Abby had gone off with this stranger without a second thought.

"Yes. They left an hour ago," Dina said.

"Tell me about these guards. Did Cade leave men to guard the house?" Luke asked, looking around. He hadn't seen anyone when he rode up.

She nodded. "But they aren't here and they're supposed to be here. I was going to ask one of them to take a note to Cook, but I couldn't see them from the house. And I've been watching for them. Sometimes they sit on the porch."

"All right. You go on inside. I'm going to have a look."

He waited until Dina had closed the door behind her before descending the porch steps and going around the side of the house. Even after he'd walked around the entire perimeter, he still hadn't seen any guards. Not sure what to make of that, he headed for the garden out back and the stables. It didn't take him long to spot the figure sprawled on the ground behind a bush, blood trickling out from a large gash on the back of his head.

He'd found one of the guards.

Chapter Twenty-Two

Cade pulled his mount up, his eyes narrowing on the road ahead. Someone was kicking up a storm of dust and moving rapidly in his direction. With a grunt of annoyance, he guided his horse off the hard-packed surface and into the grass on the side. Earlier that morning he'd divided his men into groups and sent them in a northwest direction, toward the string of hills bordering the coast. The information he'd received from the miners who were attacked made him sure the men he was hunting were still using a spot near Lillian's ranch for orphans as their main camp.

Having sent his men off, Cade had every intention of joining them in the hunt, but not until tomorrow. Tonight he intended to be with his wife.

He needed to put things right with Abagail. The sad look on her face, and her soft plea not to make her choose between him and being a doctor, had kept him awake most of the night. By the time dawn had broken over the horizon, he was convinced he'd handled the whole thing badly. He hated that she believed he expected her to give up medicine or her patients. He only wanted her to be safe. He wasn't wrong, but he wasn't right either.

He should have considered her compromise to take a guard with her whenever she needed to leave the house.

Cade sat for another few minutes, waiting. As the dust cloud drew near, the horse and rider in front of it became more distinct. Watching from under the wide brim of his hat, Cade was surprised when he recognized the man riding as if he was being chased by a pack of wolves. It was Luke Donovan, on a horse with a copper coat and pale mane. The marshal tightened his hold on the reins when his mount moved restlessly as Luke thundered closer. It wasn't until he came within a hundred feet of Cade that Luke slowed enough to make a skidding halt right next to the marshal.

"Charles sent me to find you. There's a problem with Abby," Luke said, bringing his horse right up alongside Cade's.

Alarms went off in Cade's head. "What problem? She isn't hurt, is she?"

"I don't know." Luke slid off the stallion and untied a canteen. Using his hat as a bowl, he poured water into the center and held it out in front of his mount. The animal gracefully dropped its head and made loud slurping noises as it lapped up the cool liquid.

Cade threw a leg over the back of his saddle and stepped onto the ground.

"What do you mean you don't know?" he growled, taking a menacing step forward which forced Luke to take one backwards.

"I mean I went around to the house this morning, and Miss Geraldine said she was gone."

With his gut burning, Cade took another step forward, but this time Luke stood his ground.

"Do you want to hear this, or do you want to tussle in the dirt first?" Luke asked.

The marshal stopped and clenched his hands into fists. "Explain what you're talking about and then I'll decide."

"I went by the house to deliver a note Cook sent to Abby. When I got there, Miss Geraldine was upset because Abby went off with a man who showed up at their door claiming you'd sent for her."

"Why would Abagail believe a fool story like that?" Cade demanded.

"Because the fool delivering it said you'd been shot," Luke retorted.

"What?"

Luke nodded. "Found the two guards when I went looking for them. Both knocked out, and one's badly hurt. We got

177

them into the house and Jules took the carriage horse to fetch Doc Melton."

"But Abagail's gone?" Cade's voice was hoarse and a cold sweat trickled down his spine.

"Found this stuck on a nail in the stable." Luke held out a piece of paper he'd plucked out of his shirt pocket.

Cade read it, breathing in slow and deep as he absorbed what it said. He glanced over at Luke.

"Ben Linder has her. Did Dina say what the man looked like?"

"Short, young, skinny enough he could hardly keep his gun belt up. Said his name was Tommy," Luke supplied.

"Not Linder, then. One of his men." Cade looked off in the distance, turning it over in his mind.

"It was a trick to lure me out and leave my wife alone," he said softly.

"What was a trick?" Luke asked, frowning.

"Attacking those miners. Linder knew I'd come after him." Guilt slammed hard into Cade like a boulder falling off a cliff. He'd promised to keep her safe. He should have been there. He crumpled the note in his hand.

"Note says he'll trade her for you, so at least she's still alive." Luke stopped when he was suddenly looking at Cade's back. He jumped forward and grabbed the marshal's arm. "Where are you going?"

Cade shook him off. "To get Abagail."

"But you don't know where she is. The note says he'll let you know when and where," Luke pointed out, backing up again when Cade shot him a deadly look.

"If he sent a man to get Abagail, then he's probably holed up at their main camp, waiting. That would be somewhere in the hills near Lillian's ranch. I know the way."

Luke rubbed a hand across the stubble on his chin. "You're likely right. Miss Geraldine said the man claimed you were shot halfway to that ranch with all the orphan kids.

From what she said, this Tommy sounded too dumb to think of a lie."

"Wait a minute," Luke called out when Cade started to walk away. "Charles sent his horse, Farch. He's bred for speed and stamina, but more importantly, he was raised with Marron. They're a good match. Damn few horses could catch either of them. Besides, Abby knows this horse and so does Marron. If either of them see Farch, they'll come right for you. They only have a two-hour start on you, marshal, so there's a better than good chance you can catch them before they meet up with Linder."

Cade cast a quick glance at the tall, impressive stallion standing quietly, munching on stray clumps of grass. Despite the hard run, the stallion didn't look winded. Cade withdrew the rifle strapped to his saddle and walked over to Farch. Without a word, he checked the stirrup length then stepped up into the saddle.

"Thank Charles for me," he said as he secured his rifle.

"It was Lillian's idea, so I'll thank them both. I'm going to stay at your house along with more guards, who will be inside and outside this time. If another note comes along, I'll find you. Miss Geraldine insists on staying, but Jules is with Cook over at Charlotte's house."

"I'm obliged," Cade said with a nod.

Luke grinned. "I'll bet that sticks in your craw some."

Cade let out a snort before turning Farch to the northwest. His mouth set into a grim line, the marshal headed out to find his wife.

***

"That's a right nice horse you have there, doc."

Abby half turned her head to nod and smile at her escort. They were walking their horses again because Tommy's mount was almost spent. Abby guessed the poor animal was more accustomed to pulling a wagon than having a saddle on its back.

At first she'd been so upset over the slow progress they were making, she'd alternated between wanting to scream, and simply leaving Tommy and his sad-looking horse behind. What stopped her was not knowing where to find Cade, which Tommy had refused to tell her. But it took every drop of her self-control not to let her desperate need to get to her husband overpower her common sense. But after hours of riding and listening to Tommy's constant stream of chatter, her common sense really started to take over her thoughts.

Somewhere during the long morning, what Tommy was saying finally sank into her panicked mind. Along with the growing realization that the marshal's men wouldn't have sent such a poor excuse of a messenger, with his equally run-down horse, on an urgent errand.

Then there were the lies.

When they'd first started out, Abby had asked her escort where her husband had been shot, and Tommy had said in his left leg. An hour later it was Cade's right leg. And Tommy's account of how it had happened, being ambushed and forced to run for their lives, sounded as if he admired the men who'd attacked the marshal.

There was also the matter of Cade's eyes.

To test her growing suspicions, she'd mentioned how hard it was to stand up under the stare of those brown eyes, and Tommy had whole-heartedly agreed. Anyone who'd met her husband knew his eyes were a deep, and very obvious, blue.

Five miles back, Abby had made up her mind. She had no idea why Tommy had come knocking on her door, unless one of the gang was hurt, or to draw Cade into a trap.

What she did know for sure was that Tommy had never met Cade, and so it was just as unlikely her husband was hurt and waiting for her to come save him. And she had no intention of being used as bait so they could ambush Cade, if that was the reason for this whole ruse.

Having reached those conclusions, she'd started to form an escape plan. The problem was coming up with one that allowed her to get away before Tommy could pull that revolver out of his holster.

Since she had no idea where her husband was, or if he was already on his way into a possible trap, she'd have to get out of this predicament on her own. And soon. Hopefully without getting shot.

"Maybe we should trade horses," Tommy called out. "You bein' smaller than me would be easier on my horse. We'd make better time that way, too."

Since he couldn't see her face, Abby rolled her eyes. She'd have to be as dumb as a rock to let him ride Marron.

"I'm afraid my horse is trained so nobody else can ride him," she said over her shoulder. "He'd throw you off, and then we'd only have one horse between us."

"I think I could handle him all right," Tommy said. "You just hold up for a minute."

Before she had a chance to respond, Tommy suddenly came up beside her and pointed to a hill less than a quarter mile away. "Looks like my friends have come out to meet us."

Abby lifted a hand to shade her eyes and squinted at the top of the hill. Three riders were there, silhouetted against the sky. They were too far away for her to make out their faces, but when they turned and disappeared down the backside of the hill she froze. She couldn't identify the riders, but she saw the horses well enough. Two of them had coats in a shade of brown, but the third animal was a very distinct, multi-colored gray. The same color and pattern as the horse she'd seen at the end of her street just two days ago. The one Cade had said Ben Linder was riding.

She had to get away right now, before Linder and the rest of his men reached her. Taking a deep breath, she cast a sideways glance at Tommy. Good. His attention was still on the hill and not on her. At least for the moment.

Abby carefully reached down and drew her rifle out of its holder. The soft rasp of metal against leather had Tommy's

181

gaze swinging around, but she already had the rifle up and pointed right at him as she slowly backed Marron away.

Tommy's eyes went wide. When his hand snaked down his side, Abby shook her head.

"Don't move, Tommy. Keep those hands of yours on top of your saddle." Abby said, her rifle aimed right at his chest.

After a long moment of staring at each other, Tommy suddenly laughed.

"You ain't gonna shoot me, doc."

Abby tightened her hold on the rifle. "Oh? I wouldn't be so sure of that."

He shrugged, a smirk still on his face. "I bet you've never even held that gun before, and you sure ain't never shot no one."

Abby sighed and dropped the barrel toward the ground. "You're right. I haven't."

Chapter Twenty-Three

Cade crested the hill and looked across the gently rolling landscape with its cover of grass and patches of color popping out here and there. He stepped off Farch, giving the glossy neck a firm pat as he continued to scan the countryside, searching for anything to show where the faint gunshot had come from.

A slight movement off in the distance had Cade reaching into his saddlebag. He untied the spyglass, training it on the area that had caught his interest. He slowly crisscrossed it back and forth until he found what he was looking for, a single horse and rider, eating up ground hard and fast. Cade squinted through the eyepiece, keeping it trained on the figure lying flat on the back of a big horse with a dark chocolate coat. He briefly closed his eyes and sent up a quick prayer of thanks. Marron. The horse running flat out across the grass was Marron. Cade opened his eyes and intently studied the rider. It was his wife all right, dressed in her boy clothes, with her long hair whipping about in the wind.

Fighting off the lightheaded feeling of relief cascading through him, Cade methodically backtracked with the spy glass. Three more riders came barreling over a small rise, a fair distance behind his wife, and that distance was steadily growing. Marron was definitely outrunning his pursuers. But galloping over rough terrain was dangerous business. Any horse, even one as agile as Marron, could stumble and throw a rider. He had to get to Abagail. Cade was sure she wasn't trying to control her horse, but just hanging on and letting Marron run.

Quickly gauging the angle he needed to take to intercept his wife, Cade closed the spyglass with a hard snap and leaped toward his mount. The big stallion quivered slightly as if he felt his rider's urgency. In one fluid motion Cade sent

Farch straight down the hillside, shifting his weight to help the horse keep its balance until they reached flatter ground. Without any further encouragement, the powerful animal took off in a thunder of hooves.

Cade intended to come up behind his wife and put himself between her and Linder's men, but as he drew closer, Luke's words proved true. Marron suddenly changed course and veered straight toward Farch. Cade turned and slowed the stallion until Marron caught up with them and the two horses were running side-by-side. He pulled his rifle out of its holder and swiveled in the saddle, firing several shots behind them. Linder and his men were too far away to hit, but Cade wanted them to know they were no longer chasing a lone woman. She had company.

After another half mile, Cade again turned Farch, keeping an eye to the side to be sure Marron followed. He headed straight for the same hill where he'd first spotted Abagail, skirting around the bottom until they were on the other side. Reaching over, he grabbed Marron's bridle and brought both horses to a stop, their sides heaving and coats sopping wet.

Pushing out of the saddle, he tied off the reins and grabbed the spyglass. "Stay here," he told Abby before scrambling up the small hill. Lying flat in the grass, he put the glass to his eye and scanned the countryside below. It only took a minute to locate Ben Linder and the other men with him. They'd stopped, and judging by the look of their horses, they were done. Cade figured at least one of them might have to walk back to their camp.

Smiling in grim satisfaction, he rose to his feet and made his way down the hill. Abagail was still sitting on Marron, the reins slack in her hands as she watched him. He put his rifle and spyglass away and swung up into the saddle.

"I saw a place that's a good spot to rest the horses. It's not far. Can you still ride?"

She nodded. "What about Linder and Tommy?"

"Their horses are done and so are they," Cade said, picking up his reins.

"I'm sorry, Cade."

"We'll talk about it later. Right now, we need safe cover." Cade gently kneed Farch into a walk and Marron fell into step behind him.

Not wanting to push the horses any more than they already had, it took over an hour before they reached a rise with a stand of trees along one side, and a ring of boulders on top. Cade guided Farch into the shade and dismounted. Walking over to Abby, he reached up and put his hands around her waist, lifting her off Marron's back. He set her on her feet, his hold immediately tightening when her legs buckled beneath her. Muttering a curse, Cade swept his wife into his arms and carried her over to the nearest tree, setting her down so she could lean her back against the trunk.

"I'm going to see to the horses," Cade said. "I'll be right back."

Keeping one eye on her, he quickly stripped off the saddles then led the animals to a small pool of water set under the trees. When he came back to Abagail, he had a canteen and bandanna in his hand. He knelt beside her and handed her the water. Once she'd had her fill, he soaked the bandanna and began to clean the mud off her face.

"Are you feeling all right?"

"I'm fine," Abby said.

"Good." Cade leaned over and took her face in both his hands and looked into her eyes. "Don't ever scare me like that again."

His lips came down on hers and his tongue immediately invaded her mouth. When her arms came around his neck, he pulled her close. Cade poured all the fear and terror of the last few hours into his kiss, trying without words to tell her everything he felt.

When he finally lifted his head, he pushed her hair aside and placed his lips on her ear. "Promise me, Abagail."

She buried her face in his neck and let out a sob. Startled, Cade lifted her in his arms and sat down with her in his lap, cradling her shaking body against his and running his hand up and down her back as tears ran down his shoulder, and soaked into his shirt.

"What's wrong? Are you hurt?" Cade's hands wandered down her arms and back, looking for any injury.

"No. Hold me. Please just hold me."

"Okay... Okay..." Cade's arms tightened. Figuring she was having a reaction to almost being killed, Cade brushed a gentle hand over her hair. "You're all right. You're safe now. You'll be fine."

Abby shook her head. "I know."

"Then you can stop crying, sweetheart," Cade said, dropping a kiss into her hair. "I don't like to hear you cry."

She raised a watery gaze to his. "He said you were shot. I thought I wouldn't get there in time to save you."

Cade drew in a quick breath. "You're crying because you thought I was shot? And that's why you left the house?"

Nodding, she buried her face in his shoulder. Over her head, Cade frowned. Just as he'd thought, Linder had used him to lure his wife out into the open. Anger boiled along his veins. He'd make damn sure that never happened again. And the bandit would pay for trying to get his hands on a marshal's wife. Especially his wife.

When her tears kept coming, and not knowing how to soothe her, he tried a distraction instead.

"Tell me how you got away. I heard a shot."

Abby raised her head and sniffled. Cade folded the wet bandanna until he found a fairly clean area on it before handing it to Abby. She wiped her eyes and nose, thanking him in a small voice.

"So how did you get away?" he prompted.

"I didn't shoot him, if that's what you think," Abby said.

"Him? You mean Tommy?"

She nodded. "He came to the house and said you were shot, and he would take me to you. But he couldn't remember where you were shot, and then he agreed you had very frightening, brown eyes."

"My eyes aren't brown."

"That's when I knew for sure he'd never met you so you couldn't have sent him for me. And when he saw Ben Linder, he told me his friends had decided to meet us."

Startled, Cade's mouth dropped open. "You talked to Linder?"

"No. I only saw him. He was too far away to make out clearly, but I recognized that horse he rides. So while Tommy's attention was on them, I pulled out my rifle and did what Rayne told me to do."

"What's that?" Cade asked, curious since she'd already said she hadn't shot Tommy.

"I shot up the dirt at his horse's feet. The poor animal jerked so hard, Tommy fell off. I knew Marron could outrun anything those men were riding, and he did."

She turned her head and smiled at her horse while Cade burst into laughter.

***

It was almost dark by the time they reached home again. Abby's shoulders were drooping so much Cade wasn't sure she could make it into the house. They pulled to a stop just as the door bounced open and Luke came running across the porch. He leaped down the stairs without touching a single step.

"You found her. Is she all right?"

Abby narrowed her eyes at him. "She's right here in front of you and can speak for herself." She slid off Marron and gave Luke a quick hug before handing him the reins. "Please take care of the horses. We both need food and a hot bath."

Cade came up beside her and handed Luke Farch's lead rein as well. "We'd appreciate it."

Luke eyed the two horses then looked over at Cade. "Looks like they've been through a mud storm."

"Close to it," Cade said. "Had to do a little running from Linder."

"Is he going to show up here again?" Luke frowned.

"Not likely. We ran into my men and sent them in Linder's direction. The gang's horses were pretty well done in, so I'm sure Linder won't get far before he's caught."

"That's good." Luke nodded. "I'll take care of the horses, but you're on your own from here on out." He glanced over at the porch and grinned. "You have company."

Cade turned around and peered at the porch, surprised to see a full gaggle of women leaning over the rail and staring at them. Abagail looked up as well and gave a small cry before running up the walkway. Lillian, Beth and two other women he'd never seen before quickly descended the steps, meeting his wife halfway and engulfing her in a huge hug so she disappeared from his sight.

"Good luck," Luke said, giving Cade a jaunty salute before leading the horses off toward the stable.

Cade shook his head in annoyance. He wasn't in the mood for any company. What Abagail needed was food and rest, and so did he.

Dina suddenly appeared on the porch, gripping a shawl close around her shoulders with one hand, and with the other holding onto Jules.

"Cade, is that you? Is Abby with you?" she yelled out.

"Wouldn't be standing here without her," Cade called back.

"Dina, I want to see Cade," Jules said, twisting his whole body to one side until he broke his cousin's hold.

"Oh, all right. Go on." Dina shooed the boy forward then descended the steps behind him. She marched up to the huddle of women on the walkway and loudly clapped her hands.

"Ladies. Let's go inside and have a warm drink and hear all about Abby's adventure."

"Adventure?" Cade repeated. He looked down when Jules tugged on his hand.

"When do I get to give Abby a hug?" Jules demanded.

As if by magic, the women all turned and held out their hands to Jules. Abby laughed and stepped out from the center of the group.

"I'm right here, Jules. I'd love to have that hug."

Jules raced over and threw his arms around her waist while Abby leaned over to drop a kiss on top of his head.

"Let's go in," Lillian said to nods all around.

As they made their way up the sidewalk, sweeping a grinning Jules along with them, Cade stood and shook his head. It was clear he'd have to pry his wife away from her friends.

By the time he reached the parlor they were all seated around the fireplace, pouring steaming cups of coffee and tea. Dina brought him a mug of coffee which he politely thanked her for and quickly set down before heading to the liquor cabinet. When his cousin scrunched her nose up in clear disapproval, Cade looked over at the group of women.

"Any of you ladies offended by a glass of whiskey?"

He took their laughter as permission, and poured himself a healthy portion, downing most of it in one swallow.

"Difficult day, Marshal?" Beth Davis asked, amusement weaving through her voice.

Cade raised his glass in a mock salute. "No more than usual, ma'am."

"Beth," she instantly said. "Please call me Beth."

"And I'm Maggie," the red-head with the green eyes chimed in. "I'm Ian's wife, and Luke's sister-in-law."

"We don't stand on a lot of ceremony, Marshal McKenzie, since we're all relations by blood, marriage or choice," Rayne said. "I'm Rayne Jamison. I'm married to Tremain, Charles's brother, and I hope you'll call me Rayne."

They looked at him as if they were expecting something, until it dawned on him what they were waiting for.

"I'm Cade."

"And I'm Abby," his wife quipped, making all her friends laugh and Dina smile.

Lillian nodded at Cade. "Thank you for bringing our Doctor Abby home safe and sound."

"You're welcome," Cade said. "But I was bringing my wife home. I don't want to be rude, ladies, but she needs food and rest."

Abby sighed and shook her head as she shrugged when all her friends turned to look at her. "I keep telling him I'm not a child. He doesn't need to keep giving orders about what I should or should not do."

"Like telling you to lock yourself in the house and not see your patients?" Lillian asked. "He told me that himself. And that he was going to hire guards to make sure you stayed put."

"Did he, now?" Maggie said. "Was that before or after he told Abby all about the bargain she should make, instead of givin' her a proper proposal?"

"Which leads to an interesting question. Now that she's found what's most likely the cause of Jules's problem, and I'm guessing the Linder gang is no longer a threat, does that mean the bargain is over and so is this marriage?" Beth wondered out loud.

Cade set his whiskey glass down with more force than necessary. "No, it doesn't mean that."

"I think we're all too tired to talk about this," Abby interjected.

"So do I," Dina said. "Why don't you take that bath while I fix you both something to eat?"

Lillian rose and pulled Abby up with her. "We'll help with the bath."

Before Cade knew it, his wife had disappeared upstairs with her friends and Dina had gone to the kitchen. Once the women had deserted the parlor in a flurry of skirts, he and Jules were left looking at each other. Finally his younger brother got up from the chair he was perched on and walked right up to Cade.

"I can get sick again if that'll make Abby stay."

Cade's big hand tousled his brother's hair. "We're married, Jules. She's not going anywhere."

"Jules, it's time for you to go on up to bed." Dina stood in the doorway, her hands on her hips. Once Jules had climbed the stairs, dragging his feet every step of the way, she turned to her cousin.

"Just because you're married doesn't mean she has to stay, Cade McKenzie," she said. "It might help if you told her you loved her, and asked her to stay instead of barking out orders."

"I don't bark out orders," Cade muttered. He picked up his whiskey glass and took a deep swallow.

"You do when it comes to your wife," Dina insisted. "And what about that other part? That you love her?"

Uncomfortable, Cade shifted his weight and shrugged. "That should be clear enough. She's the only woman I've chased across the countryside."

Dina's eyes softened. "Or tried to lock up because you were scared something might happen to her."

Exasperated at having that thrown back at him by every female he'd met lately, Cade glared at Dina. "There isn't a patient alive worth Abagail risking her life for, and that's what I told her."

Dina's hands were back on her hips. "Well, apparently she doesn't agree with you. Because she thought *you* were worth it, though Lord knows why. Think on that for a while, Marshal McKenzie."

With a final nod, she went back to the kitchen.

Chapter Twenty-Four

"It's wonderful, simply wonderful," Dina declared. "Our Jules hasn't had a hint of a breathing problem in over a week."

Abby watched her cousin-in-law dance her way from the stove to the pantry and back. She suspected Dina's cheerfulness was only due in part to Jules, and the other part to the gentleman sitting at the table, helping peel potatoes. When Cook glanced over at her, Abby managed a smile. She certainly had no objections if a romance developed between him and Dina. She couldn't think of two people who deserved to find love more and wished her own life was going on that happily.

"We still have to wait and watch what he eats for a while. But I'm hopeful we've discovered the cause of his ailment."

"Of course, of course. But this is the first time since we've settled in a home where he hasn't been confined to a bed. I should have realized it was something in the food I was preparing." Dina's smile dimmed. "I'll always feel guilty about causing our boy so much trouble."

Cook pointed his short-bladed knife at her. "Nonsense. How were you supposed to know some folks can't tolerate sesame seeds?"

"Maybe not. But wasn't it brilliant of Abby to get to the bottom of things?"

"Cook gets most of the credit. I read about it in a book, but he'd actually seen such a thing during his travels to the Far East," Abby said, more than willing to point out Cook's better points. She thought it must be working when Dina beamed at the man.

"Yes, he was quite impressive. But so were you, Doctor Abby," Dina declared. "Did you know what Cade said when he first mentioned you? That you were brilliant."

Abby kept her head bowed and went on scraping the skin off the potato in her hand. "Did he?"

Dina wiped her hands and walked over to the table. "Yes, he did. He thinks very highly of you, and both of us will always be grateful for what you did for Jules."

"There's no need. I'm his doctor after all," Abby said, concentrating on keeping her hand moving. When the tear escaped the corner of her eye, she bent her head even further to hide it. She didn't see the look exchanged between Dina and Cook.

"There's nothing wrong with caring about your patients," Cook said as he started to chop a potato into several large chunks. "It's fine to cry after a stressful time. It helps things get better, according to Lillian."

"Sometimes things just can't get better," Abby said, taking a quick swipe at the tear as another one took its place.

"What did he do?" Dina moved to stand beside Cook.

"Who?" The former sailor twisted around to look at her.

"My stupid cousin, of course."

Cook lowered his eyebrows. "Why is he stupid?"

"Because he's a man, and he's been upsetting Abby for the past week." Dina turned her gaze back to Abby. "What's he done?"

Giving up, Abby set her knife down and wrapped her arms around her middle. She didn't care if she was crying. Everything was awful, so why shouldn't she cry?

Cook instantly jumped to his feet. He walked around the table and gave Abby an awkward pat on the shoulder.

"I'll take care of it." When the two women stared at him, he only nodded and walked out the backdoor.

"Is he going to shoot Cade because he made you cry?" Dina asked, turning wide eyes on Abby.

193

Abby gave a weak laugh that ended in a hiccup. "Cook never carries a gun, so you don't have to worry about Cade."

"I'm not. I'm worried Cade will shoot Cook in self-defense," Dina said. "Men can be terribly stupid."

"Yes, they can be," Abby agreed. She raised the edge of her apron and dabbed at her eyes.

"So tell me what's troubling you? Aren't you and Cade getting along?" Dina asked.

Sighing, Abby looked out the window toward the stables. "It's nothing, really. We're getting along just fine. Our conversations are very polite. He tells me about his day, I tell him about mine, and we have supper together every night."

"So what's bothering you, Abby?" Dina frowned. "You sound like any married couple."

Abby closed her eyes as the tears started again in earnest. "Yes. We do. But we didn't start out like a usual married couple. We started out with a bargain. And you can't build much else on that." She stood up and gave Dina a watery smile. "I'm just being silly. I think I'll get some fresh air and go brush Marron."

"All right." Dina shook her head. *Young people can believe the most foolish things.*

***

Abby was still in the barn an hour later, running a brush over Marron's glossy coat. Depressed over the sad state of her marriage, she knew she couldn't keep putting off talking to Cade about it, but at least the tears had stopped.

"I never believed I'd see a horse that was tired of being brushed."

Abby's lips gave the barest hint of an upward turn as she glanced at her smiling cousin and the two women with her.

"You're early if you're here for the wedding party. It's not for a few hours yet. Where's Rayne?"

"Resting, according to her over-protective husband. And we brought our dresses with us," Beth said. "We came to spend time with you."

"And to be findin' out what that husband of yours did to make you cry," Maggie put in. "Cook told us. So did Dina."

Lillian moved forward and gave Abby a warm hug. "After we hear what he's done, then we can decide whether or not there's going to be a wedding party."

Maggie kicked a low bench. "Let's get a couple of these cleared off so we can be comfortable while we discuss if the marshal deserves Abby or not."

"It isn't entirely his fault," Abby said as she and Beth pushed a bench around to face the one Lillian and Maggie were working on to remove the bridles and ropes.

Beth sat and very properly arranged her skirt before pursing her lips at her friend. "Oh? What did you do to make yourself cry?"

Abby sat next to Beth and waited for Lillian and Maggie to get settled on the bench across from them.

"He only married me because of the bargain." The minute she said it, tears started flowing again.

"And now you wish it was for a different reason?" Lillian asked.

Nodding, Abby brushed a hand over her cheek. "I wish it was the same reason Charles, Ian and John married each of you."

Maggie looked at Beth and winked. "She wants him to love her."

"Abby," Lillian said gently. "I saw his face when you went to the ranch on your own. He couldn't get on his horse fast enough to go after you. And that was before the bargain."

"But that was after he'd decided I could help Jules," Abby said, her lip quivering beyond her control.

"Luke said he was sure the marshal would kill the man who kidnapped you." Maggie nodded. "I'm thinkin' that's not a man concerned over a bargain."

"But it *was* part of the bargain. His part. He promised to keep me safe," Abby argued. "And mine was to help Jules.

195

But I did that, and now he leaves the house at dawn and doesn't come back until supper, and then he leaves again after Jules goes to bed. And we barely talk."

"Are you doin' anything else when the man finally does come to your bed?" Maggie asked bluntly.

When Abby shook her head, Maggie turned to Lillian with a fierce frown.

"Did you hear that, Lillian Jamison? He's not bein' a husband at all. I'm thinkin' our Abby should come home with one of us."

"Have you talked to Cade about how you feel?" Beth asked.

Lillian leaned over and took both of Abby's hands in her own. "We're assuming you realize that you do love him, don't you?"

Abby gave her cousin's hands a gentle squeeze. It was wonderful to have her extended family around her right now, and she was sure she'd need their support after she confronted her husband. She'd already decided it would be better to face the truth than live with this agony of uncertainty. And since Cade had been avoiding her for the last week, she already knew what he was going to say.

She withdrew her hands and folded them in her lap. "I know I have to talk to him. The only way to find out how *he* feels is to ask him."

"Ask me what?"

Abby froze at the sound of the deep masculine voice behind her. She gave her friends a look she was sure conveyed the panic suddenly churning up her stomach, before slowly rising to her feet. The other three women stood up with her, and turned to face the marshal.

Lillian leaned forward and whispered into Abby's ear, "We're right here with you."

Dina came bustling into the stable, stopping halfway between Cade and Abby. "Now ladies, let's give them some time alone so they can talk things out. Come into the kitchen for a cup of coffee, or tea if you prefer."

In less than a minute she'd managed to herd the other three women outside. Abby could hear Dina's constant chatter up until the backdoor to the house closed behind her.

Cade walked over, stopping within a foot of her. Abby stared at his chest as he removed his hat and placed it on the bench. Putting one finger under her chin, Cade lifted her face to his. He studied her in silence for a long moment.

"You've been crying."

Abby shrugged. "All women do from time to time."

"I'm not interested in all women, just in you. I doubt anyone told you I've been shot, so what's made you cry?" Cade asked.

She batted his hand away. "Your being shot is not amusing, Cade McKenzie."

"I'm not laughing, Abagail McKenzie. But I'm still waiting to hear why you were crying?"

Reaching deep inside to grab a piece of courage, Abby straightened her back. She was sick and tired of their bargain. She loved him, but she would not stay with a man who didn't love her.

"I won't hold you to a marriage you don't want to be in, Cade."

Her spine stiffened even more when the man dared to smile. It seemed his manners had not improved over the past few weeks.

"I appreciate that, Abagail." Cade's eyes darkened to a shade of blue almost bordering on black. "Why would you think I don't want to be in this marriage?"

Abby took a small step backwards, prepared to throw her pride away and flee if their talk became too painful. "You only married me to help Jules, and since that's no longer a problem, you've been avoiding coming home or talking to me." Abby paused for a moment, ignoring the heat rising in her cheeks. "Or doing anything else married couples normally do."

Cade cleared his throat while Abby eyed him suspiciously. Was he laughing again? *I swear I'm going to kick him before I run to the house.*

"I need to show you something." Cade withdrew a folded piece of paper from inside his vest and handed it to her.

Abby opened it and adjusted her spectacles on her nose. After a full minute, she looked up and frowned at him. "This is the deed to the house."

"Yes, it is. I bought it for you," Cade said.

"For me?" Abby repeated slowly. "For me to live in?"

He shook his head. "No. For you to see your patients. I stopped by to see Dr. Melton a few days ago to talk over some business. He told me he's getting ready to retire and move back to his hometown in Maryland. And yesterday he sent word he'd found a buyer for his house. So, you'll be needing another place to see your patients. This house is too small for all of us, plus the kids we'll be having one day soon if I have a say about it. I thought this place would be a good size for your medical practice."

"Kids?" Abby stared up at him. "You want children?"

Cade took a step forward and ran a hand down her cheek. "I want *our* children, Abagail."

He looked around for a moment then smiled at her, his eyes lit with an inner fire. "This is the perfect spot."

Abby was so caught up in his gaze she hardly breathed. "It is?"

"As I recall, we were in a barn when I explained to you the reasons we should get married. So it's the right place to ask you to marry me." He gently cupped her face in his large hands and bent his head to place a soft kiss on her lips.

"I would have asked you the first time, but I was afraid you'd say 'no'. But now I have to ask, because I won't keep you in a marriage you don't want either, Abagail. I love you. But you need to understand that I'm a marshal. I can't promise I'll be home with you every night, and I can't promise I won't get shot now and then. But I can promise to listen to you even when I'm barking out orders, and to accept all your nosey friends into our family. I also promise to make love to you every night and any other time we can find enough privacy. To always take care of you and our children, and keep our family safe. But most of all, I promise to love you until my dying breath."

He reached into his pocket and pulled out a ring, with a large square-cut ruby in its center, surrounded by smaller diamonds.

"Marry me, Doctor Abagail Metler McKenzie," he whispered, touching his forehead to hers.

Abby tilted her head back and looked up into those deep sea-blue eyes. She thought it wasn't possible to be any happier than she was at this moment. Laying her lips on his, she kissed him until he finally lifted his head and held her off.

"Unless you want me to lay you down in the nearest haystack right now, we'd better stop." Cade's breathing was unsteady, and she could feel the trembling in his hands.

She smiled up at him and slowly ran a finger down his scar. "I would be happy to marry you, Marshal Cade McKenzie."

He drew her back into his arms and kissed her again until she was lightheaded and holding onto him to keep upright. Cade swooped her up and carried her out of the barn.

"Where are we going?" Abby gasped, her arms locked around her husband's neck.

"To tell your nosy friends we'll be late for the party, and then straight up to the bedroom to get started on those kids."

Abby laughed and laid her head on his broad shoulder. Some orders simply weren't worth arguing about.

Did you love reading about Marshal Cade McKenzie and Doctor Abagail Metler?

Be sure to pick-up the other great reads in the <u>Circle of Friends series</u>!

Be the first to receive notification of the release of the next novel in the Circle of Friends series, *Believing in Hope*. **Sign up** today at:

www.CathrynChandler.com

Follow Cathryn Chandler on your favorite media:

Facebook:
https://www.facebook.com/cathrynchandlerauthor/?fref=ts

Twitter: @catcauthor

Website/blog: www.cathrynchandler.com

If you love historical romances and romantic suspense set in the West, consider joining Pioneer Hearts—a Facebook group with over 3,700 members, both authors and readers, who love the Old West.

Pioneer Hearts:
https://www.facebook.com/groups/pioneerhearts/

Coming in July, 2017 ! *Only One Promise.* Luke Donovan is a man on a mission—to make a life and a future for himself in the gentle rolling hills of Northern California. He'd leave the gold hunting at Sutter's Creek to other men— Luke intended to build a cattle ranch. But he's one cowboy who didn't count on a determined society miss with her own dreams, and who isn't about to let Luke get in her way.

All authors strive to deliver the highest quality work to their readers. If you found a spelling or typographical error in this book, please let me know so I can correct it immediately. Please use the contact form on my website at: www.cathrynchandler.com   Thank you!

Made in the USA
Middletown, DE
08 March 2020